THE BIG BAD
DE WOLFE

HEIRS OF TITUS DE WOLFE
BOOK 2

BARBARA DEVLIN

DE WOLFE PACK: THE SERIES

By Alexa Aston
Rise of de Wolfe

By Amanda Mariel
Love's Legacy

By Anna Markland
Hungry Like de Wolfe

By Autumn Sands
Reflection of Love

By Barbara Devlin
Lone Wolfe: Heirs of Titus De Wolfe Book 1
The Big Bad De Wolfe: Heirs of Titus De Wolfe Book 2
Tall, Dark & De Wolfe: Heirs of Titus De Wolfe Book 3

By Cathy MacRae
The Saint

By Christy English
Dragon Fire

By Hildie McQueen
The Duke's Fiery Bride

By Kathryn Le Veque
River's End

By Lana Williams
Trusting the Wolfe

By Laura Landon
A Voice on the Wind

By Leigh Lee
Of Dreams and Desire

By Mairi Norris
Brabanter's Rose

By Marlee Meyers
The Fall of the Black Wolf

By Mary Lancaster
Vienna Wolfe

By Meara Platt
Nobody's Angel
Bhrodi's Angel
Kiss an Angel

By Mia Pride
The Lone Wolf's Lass

By Ruth Kaufman
My Enemy, My Love

By Sarah Hegger
Bad Wolfe on the Rise

By Scarlett Cole
Together Again

By Victoria Vane
Breton Wolfe Book 1
Ivar the Red Book 2
The Bastard of Brittany Book 3

By Violetta Rand
Never Cry de Wolfe

Titles by Barbara Devlin

DEDICATION

As with Lone Wolfe, my first contribution to Kathryn Le Veque's Kindle World of De Wolfe Pack, I can't possibly dedicate this book to anyone other than my dear friend Kathryn. I could say all manner of things, heap all sorts of praise, and gush, but I believe I will simply say I love Kat.

TABLE OF CONTENTS

CHAPTER ONE

London

June 17

The Year of Our Lord, 1497

A BLOODY BUSINESS, war knew no limits, as the mortal distinctions of rank, privilege, and power meant naught in the heat of battle, and death struck with indiscriminate and arbitrary abandon. Beneath a clear blue sky, the Cornish soldiers approached, and enemies clashed. It was in the center of the action that Arsenius Titus De Wolfe, sitting tall atop his destrier, charged an unfortunate foe.

A lancer like his father, a legendary warrior and one of the fiercest knights in the kingdom, Arsenius leveled his weapon and heeled the flanks of his mighty stallion, and he caught his adversary in the cuirass, which knocked the rebel to the ground. In truth, theirs was not a fair fight, as His Majesty's troops exceeded the opposition in numbers, skill, and armaments.

After King Henry VII penalized the Stanneries, in relation to a conflict regarding tin-mining regulations, and levied a tax to pay for the costs associated with the war against the Scots, for which the Cornish assumed a disproportionate share given the border incursions did not impact Cornwall, tempers flared and an uprising was born. What no one expected was that some fifteen thousand combatants would band together and march, for all intents and purposes, unopposed from Taunton to the King's threshold at the Deptford Strand Bridge.

Thither would be hell to pay for that.

But his immediate concern focused on the forward assault up the middle, under the command of Lord Daubeney, as two other royal compliments directed by Lords Suffolk, Oxford, and Essex flanked either side, and Arsenius waved to his armiger. "Follow me."

Just then, a hulking figure of a knight advanced in Arsenius's wake, and he flicked the reins of his destrier and set a blazing pace, with the impressive soldier, which harkened a comparison to one of Alaric's Visigoth mercenaries who brought the Roman Empire to its knees, bringing up the rear. Given so many enemy combatants lacked a horse, he dropped his lance, slid from the saddle, and drew his sword.

Likewise, the huge fighter halted his steed, leaped to the ground, and unsheathed two lightweight blades forged of Damascus steel.

"Must you always make such a grand entrance?" Arsenius snickered. "As you appear better suited for the stage, cousin."

"You are one to talk." Titus De Wolfe, son of Atticus, the Lion of the North and the patriarch of the estimable family descended of the great William De Wolfe, and Isobeau, adopted a defensive posture. "And why do you not bare your face, as that alone would scare off half of them?"

"Are we not the witty sort? And your lady declared otherwise when I rode her this morrow." As was their way, Arsenius turned on his cousin, more a brother in light of their years, and back-to-back, they confronted the enemy hoard. "How many would you estimate?"

"Perchance, two to three hundred souls in our immediate vicinity. Hardly seems fair." Wearing the signature De Wolfe ailette attached to his pauldron, in much the same fashion as Arsenius, Titus nudged Arsenius's shoulder. "Are you ready?"

"Aye." In anticipation of the fight, Arsenius bent at the knees. "Let us play, cousin."

And so it began. Moving as a single entity, given they stood at equal height; Arsenius and Titus launched a brutal offensive against their foes, more farmers than professional soldiers. Each manifested an imposing adversary on his own merit, but combined the larger-than-life relatives presented an infallible example of human prowess no opponent could challenge with any semblance of hope for success. When Arsenius moved right, his brash relation veered left in a savage but precise dance of death that spared no rebel, and one by one the enemy fell to the devastating De Wolfe duo.

Joined at the hip for as long as he could remember, Arsenius and Titus were evenly matched in every way, excepting their technique. Trained in Cypress, where he served alongside *le Dauphin*, Titus executed a singular, lethal style he mastered in tutelage by the Turks, whereas Arsenius deployed the traditional *botta-in-tempo* and *coup de main*, but the result was the same as they ravaged the Cornish troops.

Beneath a brilliant golden blanket, as the sun continued its journey across the sky, body after body hit the ground with a thud until the Cornish signaled their surrender. By dusk, countless casualties littered the landscape, and Arsenius doffed his bassinet and rubbed his eyes.

"This was no battle." He choked on the familiar stench of damp earth mixed with blood, sweat, and tears of the injured and the dying. "It was a massacre."

"I agree." After yanking off his helm, Titus wiped his forehead and spat. "Thither is no honor in such foul work."

"Sirs Arsenius and Titus, His Majesty summons you." The armiger peered toward the verge. "The King bade you appear with haste."

"Now what have you done?" Arsenius chucked Titus's chin.

"I have been with you the entire time." With a snort of unveiled disgust, Titus shifted his weight. "How do you know the fault is mine?"

"Past experience." Shaking his head, Arsenius sifted through brief recollections of their shared history. "Were you not the one who seduced the Queen's favored consort on Shrove Tuesday, no less, which almost landed us a date with His Majesty's executioner?"

"You neglect to mention Lady Margaret, in the heat of passion, confessed a nefarious plot to overthrow the

Crown, for which you and I were later knighted. How did the King put it?" Narrowing his stare, Titus snapped his fingers. "Ah, yes. We are most right and true men in dedicated service to England, and who am I to argue the Sovereign's assessment?"

Arsenius reflected on her sword-wielding, curse-spitting spouse and grimaced. "And when it came to Lady Margaret, you were quite dedicated to service."

With a cat-that-ate-the-canary grin, Titus winked and climbed into the saddle of his destrier. "Indeed, I was, as I pursued her for months, but you are one to talk, after your bare-arsed jaunt through the royal stables, whither Lord Tabarant caught you grinding his wife's corn."

"That was a momentary lapse in judgment for which I have endeavored to atone." Yet Arsenius savored the recollection, and despite his best attempts, he yielded to mirth as he reclaimed his steed. "Who knew that old, gotch-gutted, cream-faced loon could run so fast?"

"Well, in all fairness, you had your breeches and chausses gathered about your knees, which slowed your escape." Slapping his thighs, Titus howled with laughter. "That was a sight I shall never forget, and I must say I feared for your future heirs, when you fled through the topiary garden with the thorny hedgerows."

"Cousin, believe me, I scared myself." Wincing, he revisited the vicious wounds in odd places, which he could not quite explain to the physic, and tried but failed to erase the painful memory from his brain, as he returned to his saddle. "Yet we always manage to survive, because we support each other in our adventures."

"And just what manner of adventure do you have in mind?" As they galloped toward the royal tent, Titus cast a glance at Arsenius. "Ah, but I know you too well. What is her name?"

"Does it matter?" He shrugged, as his stallion soared up the hillside. "What say we celebrate our victory with some of our favorite ale and fare?"

"Blonde, brown, raven, or redhead?" Titus urged his mount faster. "Or does it matter?"

"One should never rush such an important decision." The King's guards stood at attention, as Arsenius and Titus neared. "But I believe I shall let Fate make that decision for me."

"Ah, a gambling man." Mid-chuckle, Titus sobered.

"Look yonder. Your father awaits."

"That is not good." Arsenius peered at his sire and waved as he slowed his destrier. "Papa, we bested the rebels and won the battle."

"I would not be too sure about that." The elder Titus frowned. "Come to my tent, as we have much to discuss."

Just then, the King shouted at some unknown, unfortunate soul. "We are not pleased that several thousand rebels marched to our doorstep, unimpeded, and we would have blood in recompense."

"Hurry." Father flicked his fingers, and Arsenius led his horse to the back of the line. "Step inside my temporary accommodation, as I require privacy."

"What is wrong?" Curious, Arsenius glanced at his cousin, who arched a brow. "We successfully defended London against the Cornish attackers. Why is the Crown angry?"

"Do you really need me to answer that question?" On a table, Father rolled up a map, tossed it aside, grabbed a chair, and sat. "I suggest you take your ease, my son, as what I have to say will, no doubt, shock you."

"Aye, sir." For as long as Arsenius could remember,

when Father used the general reference, storm clouds loomed on the horizon. "Am I in trouble?"

"That is putting it mildly." Father rolled his eyes. "And when your mother finds out what happened, my neck will be in peril."

"I do not understand." Glancing at the younger Titus, who shrugged, Arsenius revisited the events of the day; sifting through his actions in search of an unintended err to explain his sire's gloomy demeanor and avoid a date with the executioner. "If I offended His Majesty, in any way, I will apologize."

"You mistake my meaning." With a sigh, Father bent, opened his trunk, and retrieved a bottle, and Arsenius realized the situation was grave if it drove his sire to drink. "Given your heroic performance on the battlefield, in defense of the realm, the Crown has bestowed upon you an earldom and a prosperous seigneury in Cornwall."

"What of my deeds, which were equally coura-geous?" Titus inquired. "Is my sacrifice to be ignored?"

After a healthy draw from the bottle, Father wiped his mouth and said, "The King also bequeaths a wife."

"Great abyss of misery." Titus burst into uncon-trolled mirth. "But you may take your reward, as I covet it not."

"I would not be too quick to delight in Arsenius's difficulty." Father scratched his jaw. "As the King bequeathed the same to you."

"What?" Titus flinched.

"Now who is laughing?" Slumping forward, Arsenius propped an elbow on the table and cupped his chin. "But Mama will never support a union in which she had no say in the selection."

"Trust me, between your mother and His Majesty, I would rather confront the King, as naught scares me more than Desi's temper." To Titus, Father said, "And Atticus may kill me, when we apprise him of the not so felicitous developments, given he and Isobeau are to host the weddings at the Lair."

"Well that should be interesting." Arsenius reflected upon that gem of brilliance and shuddered. "Thither could be violence."

"No, that will not happen." Father pinned Arsenius with a steely glare. "Whatever their station, our future in-laws will be De Wolfes."

"I understand, father." Arsenius glanced at his cousin, who blanched. "But at present they remain the enemy."

THE SUN PEEKED above the horizon, and the heavens kissed the earth on an unusually warm morning, as Lady Senara Arscott stood before the lancet window and admired the lush green countryside of Cornwall. Born and raised on the rugged, wild moorlands of England, she loved the quaint town of Penryn, situated on the river bearing its name.

Descended of a long line of Arscotts, who could trace their ancestry to the fourth century, when that part of the kingdom was called *Belerion*, or Land's End, she took great pride in her estimable heritage. Like the motto upon which the city had been founded, *Onen hag oll*, One and all, she spent her days in preparation for a future that would uphold the traditions of her ancestors and her family legacy.

"Senara, you waste valuable time." Mama clapped her hands. "We must complete the hem of your gown, and the situation is urgent, given your wedding to Petroc is in a fortnight."

"But Father and Petroc have not returned from London." And that nagging fact kept her awake in the dark hours, as the men should have arrived days ago, but they had nary a word of the Cornish troops or their fate. "While I am ready to do my duty, and of my own free will I have given my vow of filial obedience, I cannot marry without the groom."

"Still, you should not delay, as I gather Petroc is anxious to make you his bride." Mama continued her work, assessing a stitch with discriminating scrutiny. "After all, you have been betrothed from the cradle. Are you not equally excited?"

"Of course, I am happy to fulfill my commitment." Shrugging, she strolled to her chair, sat, retrieved a needle and thread, and tugged on the opposite end of the skirt of the rich burgundy giornea. Although she gave every appearance of calm, on the inside, she could not quiet her internal unrest. "However, I consider Petroc more a friend than a husband, when I had hoped to form an attachment based on love. Is it wrong to want more? What am I to do, Mama?"

"You would do well to focus on providing a male heir to carry on our legacy and forget such nonsense regarding an emotional connection, as that is not the purpose of the sacrament." With a commanding and enviable posture, which Senara had seen on occasions too numerous to count and made it clear the topic was not open for discussion, Mama resumed her task and set another perfect stitch. "For a woman, procreation is the sole intent of a union."

"What of happiness?" In a rush, Senara pricked her finger and winced. "Wherefore is it written that I must temper my expectations to suit society?"

"It is known, my dear." At last, Mama secured her needle and peered at Senara. "It is unwise to wish for something more. At best, you might hope for amiable companionship. Otherwise, you court naught but despair and heartbreak."

"Is that what happened to you?" Despite their difference of opinion, Senara always heeded her mother's advice, as Mama was well-respected in the community. "Forgive me, but I have long suspected you do not love Papa."

"That is because I entered the union with no unreasonable requirements, much to my satisfaction, and I recommend you follow my path." How sad it seemed that Mama settled for less than a true and devoted bond even as she proclaimed her contentment. "Your father and I were strangers when we wed, as is often the case, thus you are fortunate to know Petroc. It will make your first night as husband and wife much easier."

"Ah, yes." A startling image formed in her mind, bodies intertwined in the mating dance, and she shuddered, given Mama had explained the process of marital relations in startling detail bereft of any hint of the pleasure to be gained therein, leaving Senara both fascinated and terrified of the singular event. "I forgot about the consummation."

"Just remember my counsel." Mama wagged a finger. "Lie back, close your eyes, and permit him to complete his occupation, and it will go easier if you do not fight him. And the sooner you produce an heir, the sooner he will seek his jollies elsewhere, and you may live in peace."

"That sounds dreadful." And if Petroc intended to avail himself of other women, he would do so without his most prized part of his anatomy, as Senara would not tolerate such an affront.

"On the contrary." With an unveiled expression of pride, Mama lifted her chin and smiled. "Ryol and I have formed a lasting friendship, and I have you and your sister, so thither have been compensations. Also, my position has afforded me the chance to help our citizens. If you are smart, and you are smart, that is whither you will make your mark."

A knock at the door snared Senara's attention, and she said, "Come."

"My lady, a small group of riders approaches from the east." Lowen, the steward, crossed to the lancet window. "I believe it is his lordship."

"But—you said a small group?" Senara dropped her gown, ignored her mother's ensuing tsk, and rushed to the ledge. "Papa took five hundred men from our garrison to fight His Majesty's unfair taxes."

"Given the size of the party, it would appear his lordship met disaster, Lady Senara." Frowning, the grey-haired steward wiped his brow. "And my son was among those who answered the call to arms."

"Let us not rush to conclusions, Lowen." Yet she gulped as the staggering collective of some twenty persons neared the gate, and she feared the obvious. "Shall we repair to the courtyard and greet our heroes?"

"Do not tarry, as they may need care." Mama hurried into the hall. "Lowen, summon the physic."

"Aye, my lady." The steward rushed into the passage and veered left in the entryway.

All but running, Senara lifted her skirts and joined

the others, who gathered to welcome those who defended Cornwall from the King's tyranny. When she spied Papa at the fore, a casual glance revealed the lines of strain and the stony, taut lips about his usually affable countenance, which conveyed a wealth of meaning that left her trembling.

Her family was in trouble.

"Ryol." With outstretched hands, Mama darted into Papa's embrace. "What happened? Whither art our soldiers?"

"Those who were not killed in battle were taken into custody, but His Majesty promised to let them come home, if I abide by the terms of surrender, and I will do so." In an instant, Papa drew up short. "Senara, I will speak with you in the solar, now." Trudging past the guards, her father stormed into the grand entry and yelled at a servant, "Bring some wine to my chamber."

"Father, what is wrong?" Senara skipped in his wake, daring to ponder what altered his manner. "If we lost the fight, but the Crown spares our troops, then we have still won, have we not? Wherefore are you so unsettled?"

"The taxes must be paid, and I am forthwith stripped of my title, but thither is more the King demands, in light of our rebellion." In the family gathering room, Papa doffed his tabard, sat in his usual chair, bent forward, and cradled his head in his hands. "And His Majesty claims Bellesea and my firstborn child as the spoils of war."

"No, Ryol. I can tolerate a great many things, but I cannot countenance the trade of my child, as if she were no more than a piece of meat." In that moment, Mama dropped to her knees and rested her palms to Father's thighs. "Never have I asked you for anything, never have I disobeyed you, but I beg you, not my baby. We can find another home, but we cannot replace our daughter. Thither is no other way?"

"What would you have of me, Wenna? Should I revolt and refuse a royal command, for which the Sire will surely see my head on a pike, mayhap with yours, and orphan both our offspring, to have them snatched by the Crown, in the end?" Papa gazed at Senara and flicked his fingers. "Come hither, girl."

"Yes, Father." Given no opportunity to digest the inauspicious developments, which boded ill tidings, Senara clung to her wits. Thither would be time for panic and tears, later. When Papa clutched her wrist with a steely grip, she winced. "You are hurting me,

Father."

"I am sorry, Senara." He eased his hold. "But you are our only hope for survival."

"Tell me what you need from me, and I will do it." If only her voice carried the strength and courage of conviction, but she vowed to persevere. "As an Arscott, I am at your service and stand ready to obey His Majesty's orders."

"You are a dutiful daughter and a credit to your sex, and I have never been more proud. Much is required of you, and I would mitigate the circumstances, if I could, but I cannot divert the Sovereign, so you must be brave, my girl." After brushing aside Mama, Father scooted from his seat and stretched tall. Framing Senara's face, he kissed her forehead, and the tender display almost brought her low. "The King gives you in marriage to one of his knights, along with the title and Bellesea."

"*No.*" Mama shrieked in unmasked horror. "Can you not protest, Ryol? Whither are we to go? How are we to live?"

"And what of my betrothal to Petroc?" Fear—no, sheer terror shivered down her spine, and Senara realized a cruel twist of fate forced her to confront the same situation as her mother. If only her future husband was as kind as her father. "I am to wed a stranger, a man about whom I know naught?"

"What would you have me do, Wenna? Should we wait until His Majesty puts our necks on the block, that the Crown might seize both our children?" Papa inquired of Mama. To Senara, he said, "But if we acquiesce, you will be a countess, and you will remain at Bellesea, so you must promise to guard our people against those who would harm them, as I am unable to protect them from His Majesty's wrath. Remember what you were taught, and do not shame your mother and I."

"Of course, Father, but what of you, Mama, and Ysella?" Senara fretted for her younger sister, who, by the Lord's grace, survived a wicked bout of consumption and struggled with her health. "What is to become of you?"

"We are at the mercy of the new lord of Bellesea." Tipping her chin, Papa brought her stare to his. "Perchance you might soften his heart, and secure his permission for us to live on the estate. As the official producer of the King's clotted cream, I have some value to your new fiancé, and our methods are a great secret I will carry to my grave."

"How am I to persuade a man of which I possess no knowledge to bend in my favor?" The weight of the world settled on her shoulders, as she pondered a future that no longer existed and new prospects that could yield naught but misery, for her and her kin. As always, Senara mulled the possibilities, her mind raced in various directions, and she scrambled to devise a plan that would spare her family. "What do you know of him, and when is the wedding to take place?"

"We depart inland to the Scottish village of Wolflee, on the morrow, and the ceremony will commence the day after our arrival at the Lair." Papa pressed a fist to his mouth, and tears welled in his blue eyes, which only compounded her anxiety. "And the brute who claims you as his property, in reward for killing untold numbers of our fellow Cornishmen, is named Arsenius De Wolfe."

CHAPTER TWO

N AUGHT COULD INSPIRE fear more than four pedestrian words, when considered on their own, but taken together as a whole their meaning incited a wealth of angst and apprehension in the most valorous warrior, *His Majesty summons you.* In the past, Arsenius met the various dates with destiny in the spirit intended, with courage and conviction, unaware of the outcome, understanding full well that the royal audience could be his last. Of course, it was easy to stand fast, confident of his survival, as he never acted in haste or against the Sovereign, and a steady stream of rewards bolstered his equanimity. In all his imaginings, and he courted some wild reveries, never had an arranged marriage entered his thoughts, and he viewed his bride-to-be as more a penance than a boon.

"Could you not have prevented this mess?" Atticus raked his fingers through his hair and groaned, as he paced the solar. "Mayhap a generous payment, of some sort, to appease the King's thirst for wealth?"

"Uncle, believe me, I tried everything to spare our sons, but thither was naught I could do to avoid the matches, and you know how the Sire can be when he is provoked." Smacking a fist to a palm, Father shook his head. "By God's bones, His Majesty was furious that so many rebel troops marched on London, unopposed, which exposed a dangerous weakness in the Crown's political connections that no leader could afford. These unions are about power, not a felicitous match."

"This is all your fault." Mama stomped a foot. "And if my baby is injured in the process, the King will answer to me, and I will never forgive you."

With a familiar pained expression, Papa shuffled his feet. "But, sweetheart—"

"Do not 'sweetheart' me, you great abyss of incompetence." Mama gave vent to a telltale sob of woe, which never failed to bring Papa to his knees.

Uncle Atticus laughed, until Isobeau wrapped an arm about Mama's shoulders. "Prithee, just what do you find so humorous, given my angel faces a similar forced wedding?" That quieted Atticus in similar resplendent fashion, and Arsenius vowed never to let a woman manipulate him in such an embarrassing manner. "And if you do not seize upon a means to resolve the predicament to our satisfaction, you may retire to the garrison, and sleep with the soldiers for the remains of your days."

Ever since their arrival at the Lair, the imposing ancestral pile of the De Wolfes, Father and Atticus had argued without pause, while Mama and Isobeau wept one minute and quarreled with their respective husbands in the next instance, thus no one enjoyed any peace.

Hugging the wall, Arsenius glanced at his cousin, who peered at the exit. As the elders fought, with Mama and Isobeau posing a united front against their husbands, Arsenius and Titus crept from the room. In the hall, Titus exhaled and rolled his eyes.

"Never have I seen Mama so angry." Titus tugged at his doublet and whistled. "And to my recollection, the only occasion upon which she banished Father from her bed was after the feast of Christmastide in London, when he danced with Lady Arweld, but that period of atonement lasted but a small portion of an evening, as they woke the entire household when they reunited."

"I remember that." Arsenius scratched his chin.

"Did not the King order Atticus to indulge Lady Arweld?"

"He did." Titus narrowed his stare. "Do you really think that makes a difference when, as is the case with Desiderata and your sire, Mama reigns supreme, whither Father is concerned."

An eerie sensation traipsed his soul, and Arsenius shivered. "We must never let that happen to us."

"Agreed." As if plagued by the same affliction, Titus rubbed the back of his neck and then slapped Arsenius on the shoulder, as they navigated the narrow passage. "Let us search out a firkin of ale in which to drown our sorrow."

"Cousin, you are wise beyond your years." In the great hall, Arsenius hailed a servant, requested their drink of choice, and sat at a table near the back of the large gathering room. "Have you reviewed the condition of your new estate?"

"Nay." As usual, Titus delayed his duties. "I suppose I shall survey the situation when I arrive in Cornwall, but I wager you have scrutinized every detail of the reports we received."

"Wherefore would you say that?" Of course, Arsenius had combed over each page of the documents assessing the status of Bellesea.

"History." A maid delivered two tankards of ale, curtseyed, and excused herself. "I know you too well, cousin." Titus raised his mug in toast. "To your marriage."

"And to yours." Arsenius consumed a healthy draft and belched. "After studying the monetary impact of the King's tariffs, I understand why the Cornish farmers rebelled. They shoulder the greatest portion of the tax burden for a war that benefited them not, while His Majesty demands Lord Arscott supply the usual amount of clotted cream to appease the royal appetite. The situation is beyond unreasonable."

"Careful, Arsenius." Titus peered over either shoulder and frowned. "The walls have ears, and you could still land in the stocks."

"I know, but I sympathize with my soon-to-be in-laws." Reflecting on the difficult task looming on the horizon, Arsenius scratched his chin. "They have forfeited their ancestral lands, their title, their industry, and their legacy. No doubt, they hate us, yet we are to wed one of their women. Their loss is our gain, and I would not rub their noses in their misery. Rather, I would welcome them."

"What do you propose?" Leaning forward, Titus propped his elbows on the table. "Most assuredly, they will hate us."

"Who could blame them?" For a while, Arsenius revisited the various events precipitating the hasty nuptials, and then he recalled his upbringing and the words branded in his memory. "The answer is simple. We are De Wolfes."

"And De Wolfes always take care of our own." Smiling, Titus nodded. "How could I forget, when Papa recited that every day of the first twenty years of my life?"

"Although His Majesty considers our brides the enemy, the betrothals define them as family, and we must treat them as such." But how should he make the initial overture? "It is imperative we reassure our future wives that we are not their adversaries. Indeed, we are their allies and protectors."

"How do you suggest we achieve our goal, while seizing their birthright and their maidenhead?" Titus arched a brow. "Trust me, I am not sure which scares me more or presents the greater danger."

"Do not fool yourself." All manner of wild imaginings filled his brain. "The latter poses the most formidable threat, and I have no clue whither to begin, as I have never, to my knowledge, deflowered a virgin. Have you any experience with such creatures?"

"Bleeding balls of agony, no." Titus wrinkled his nose. "I prefer skilled ladies, as opposed to chaste innocents, and I dread the time and energy we must expend to teach them the ways of pleasure. The poor thing will probably collapse in a fit of hysteria upon glimpsing my longsword."

"Mayhap we should inquire after our fathers for counsel, as they faced the same quandary on their wedding night." Even as Arsenius voiced the suggestion, he trembled. "Although I am not eager to broach the topic, as I anticipate a series of endless baiting, taunting, and feminine giggles."

"That is because their fair temperament hinders their ability to engage in serious topics." Pointing for emphasis, Titus snickered. "In fact, my father contends that every discussion of import with my mother ends in bed."

"No doubt the female penchant for emotion hinders their judgment, as I suspect the same is true of Mama." An odd symphony of sighs, moans, and groans played in his ears, and Arsenius quivered. He was but a lad when he discovered the source of the strange noises, as his parents made love in a stable at Braewood Castle, and he wished he could erase the disturbing vision from memory. "Papa often laments similar situations with my mother. Perchance physical relations offer the sole means of consolation when real world issues invade my mother's gentle existence, and she cannot cope."

"Well, we are the stronger sex." Titus nodded in agreement. "We would do well to take notes for future reference, that we might provide succor in like fashion. You know me, I will take any excuse to drain my moat."

"Oh, do I know you." Laughing, Arsenius stared at the contents of his tankard. "I wonder if I might ask you a personal question."

"When have you not?" Titus snorted. "We have no secrets, cousin. I am your brother, as you are most assuredly mine."

"I wondered if you embrace the opportunity the King bestowed upon us?" Thus Arsenius exposed his inner feelings. Indeed, he could tell Titus anything without fear of criticism. "Do you never find yourself alone amid our family? Are you never lost in the crowd? Have you ever wished that you might journey some place whither—"

"—No one knows my name?" With an expression of understanding and sympathy, Titus locked forearms with Arsenius. "Whither no one has heard of the De Wolfe legacy?"

"Aye." Arsenius should have known Titus could comprehend the awesome responsibility that came with affiliation with one of England's oldest and most respected noble families. "Forgive me, if this offends you, but I am excited about the prospect of moving to Cornwall and forging my own heritage. And although I do not yet know the character of my bride-to-be, I am emboldened by the possibilities associated with the title and estate."

"I, too, am blessed with renewed vigor and a spirit of adventure I have not experienced since Father hired my first whore." Titus slapped his thighs. "Ah, I have fond recollections of her red hair and the funny little sounds she made in the throes of passion. What was she called?"

"How should I know?" Compressing his lips, Arsenius averted his gaze. "And I wager her passion relied more on Atticus's generous payment than your fledgling abilities between the sheets."

"Do not insult my skills, cousin." Titus sobered. "Though you have grown to equal my size, I can still whip you."

"Is that so, old man?" Arsenius downed the last of his ale, set down the tankard with a loud thud, and stood. "I would like to see you try."

In the blink of an eye, Titus lunged across the table and grabbed Arsenius by the throat. Moving swift and sure, Arsenius tripped his foe, and they toppled to the ground. Rolling left and then right, with each gaining the high ground for a moment, before the other made a successive launch, they knocked over and reduced a bench to splinters, chuckling the entire time. Titus rumpled Arsenius's hair, and he pinched his cousin's nose, until someone coughed rather loudly.

"What goes on hither?" Folding his arms, Atticus glared at his son and then Arsenius. "It appears a couple of braying asses have ventured into the great hall."

"Mayhap a visit to the sanctuary and an afternoon spent in reflective prayer will do them some good." Adopting a similar portentous stance, Father bared his teeth. "But first my son will right his clothing and comb his hair, that he might greet his future wife in a manner befitting a De Wolfe, as her traveling party is just arrived."

TALES OF THE renowned beauty of Scotland preceded Senara's long and tortuous journey to the border village of Wolflee, the site of the Lair, her intended's ancestral home, but naught could have prepared her for the breathtaking, watercolor sunsets that provided a majestic backdrop for the lush, green highlands. And occupying a dominating pride of place in the shadow of Wolflee Hill, like some great sentry, as if the inhabitants sought to boldly declare no need of a geographical advantage, sat the impressive stronghold of the De Wolfe's.

Composed entirely of dark grey sandstone, the castle boasted the tallest curtain wall she had ever seen, decorated with frieze carved parapets featuring morose gargoyles, and crenellated towers soared toward the heavens to kiss the clouds. After crossing the primary bridge, the caravan paused before wrought iron portcullis of the barbican.

"Yonder who goes?" a guard inquired of Papa.

"Lord—er, that is to say, I am Ryol Arscott, father of Senara Arscott, betrothed of Sir Arsenius De Wolfe." So much had changed in so little time, and even her father required a reminder of his new status, which stripped him of his heritage, robbed him of his rank, and reduced him to an untitled pauper. "I believe His Grace, Titus De Wolfe expects us."

"Of course, Lord Arscott." When the guard addressed her father with respect and bowed, Papa stood upright, and she almost cried as she glimpsed the pride absent of late. "Welcome to the Lair. The honorable Sir Atticus De Wolfe awaits your arrival in the bailey."

Nearing the end of her voyage and life, as she knew it, she fought tears. What had once been a joyous event, the joining of two long-allied families, had become a source of sadness, and the trip better resembled a funeral procession than a wedding celebration. Again and again, her father reasserted the need for cooperation and acquiescence. As she steered her gentle mount into the inner courtyard, she almost choked on the lump in her throat, when she spied her new relations assembled in a receiving line.

While the elegantly garbed ladies smiled, the men caught Senara's attention, and everything in her wanted naught more than to turn around and ride for Cornwall. Giants all, the male De Wolfe's were best characterized as mountainous structures with irresistibly handsome attributes. But which of the imposing figures was her future husband?"

The party dismounted, and Senara took her position behind and to the right of her father. A particular De Wolfe gazed upon her as if he knew how she looked without her chemise, and she sniffed and lifted her chin, quietly but pointedly admonishing his rude behavior. How dare he stare at her before they were formally introduced?

"Lord Arscott, I am Atticus De Wolfe." The distinguished gentleman extended a hand, which Papa accepted. "As the head of the family, it is my privilege to welcome you to the Lair." He stepped to the side. "Allow me to present my wife, Isobeau and my son, Sir Titus. This is my nephew, His Grace, Titus De Wolfe, the Duke of Ausborn, Her Grace, Desiderata, and their eldest son, Sir Arsenius."

Senara gulped, as she may have already piqued the ire of her groom. When she offered a smile as an olive branch, of a sort, Arsenius winked. Oh, the impudence.

"Your Grace." Papa bowed. "Permit me to introduce my wife, Wenna, my daughter, Senara, and my youngest, Ysella."

Even beneath the weight of her traveling gown, she executed a perfect curtsey.

"Lord Arscott, I am more sorry than I can convey over the inauspicious affairs that necessitated this meeting." Her soon-to-be in-law possessed kind eyes and a tranquil manner. "Prithee, know that I did everything in my power to mitigate the retributive justice enacted by His Majesty. However, as we are to be family, know that you now enjoy the protection and support of the De Wolfes."

"Let us not talk of the unpleasantness, when thither are friendships to be solidified prior to tomorrow's nuptials." Her Grace, a beauteous lady blessed with patrician features and a commanding air of refinement, clutched her husband's arm. "Shall we repair to the great hall for refreshments, that you might take your ease after your lengthy travels?"

"How were the roads?" Atticus ushered them into a grand entry, whither they shed their outerwear. "The rains have been heavy, of late."

"They were a terrible mess and slowed us down, as we did not want to risk injury to the horses," Papa explained.

As the parents gathered about a large table, the hosts surprised her by foregoing their positions of prominence at the massive dais, choosing instead to sit with the visitors, and that boded well in Senara's estimation, as it suggested they viewed their new relations as equals.

At one end, she led Ysella to a chair. "Are you all right, sister?"

"Do not worry about me, Senara." Ysella pressed the back of her hand to her cheek. "I am fine. Just a tad tired."

"Would you like some ale or wine, my lady?" A servant drew two mugs from a tray. "Or would you prefer something hot? Mayhap, tea?"

"Tea sounds lovely, gramercy." To her amazement, Arsenius and the younger Titus, thither was a story in that name, she would wager her life on it, occupied the seats opposite her, and Senara ignored them.

But she could not disregard their incessant whispers and snickering, which boiled her blood. And she wanted to rattle the rooftops, when Titus said in a low voice, "Not bad, cousin. I hope I am as fortunate with my bride."

That was it, she had reached her limit of feminine deportment, and just as she was about to take issue with Arsenius and his brash relative, Ysella coughed and stood. "May I retire to my accommodation, as I am exhausted, Father?"

"I am remiss in my duties." Isobeau clapped her hands, and another servant stepped to the fore. "Prithee, show Lady Ysella to her chamber."

"Shall I go with her, Papa?" Senara peered at Arsenius, who cast a lopsided grin. "Ysella might need my help."

"No." Father shook his head. "You should avail yourself of the opportunity to speak with your intended and become acquainted, as you are more than adequately supervised."

That was the last thing on her mind, as her fiancé appeared to wrestle with laughter at her predicament, and she swallowed an unladylike curse. Clasping her hands in her lap, at last, she met Arsenius's gaze, and she clenched her gut.

Piercing in their intensity, his crystal blue eyes, thickly lashed, the highlight of a beauteous chiseled visage framed with thick brown hair, and arrogant smile bespoke myriad naughty thoughts, all of which she pretended not to notice, but her cheeks burned with embarrassment.

"My, but your blush is charming, Lady Senara." Of course, her tormentor had to remark on her discomfit, and she bit her bottom lip against a dagger-sharp retort. "Ah, you are thinking of a word, but do not tell me. Let me guess." He tapped his chin and snapped his fingers. "Has it something in common with a winter frost?"

Again and again, she recited her promise in her head, as she could not risk alienating Arsenius, and a single acrimonious comment could render her family homeless. So, despite every instinct shouting at her to respond, to engage in verbal warfare, she held her tongue.

"And still she remains quiet." Arsenius frowned and leaned forward to impart in a whisper, "Your bosom is quite tempting, and I cannot wait to explore your bounty after our wedding."

Warmth seeped into her chest and spread to her limbs, as her ears pealed a carillon of alarm, but she clung to her wits. How she ached to yield and set the crude brute on his heels, but her pledge silenced her protests.

"Well done, my dear." Titus snorted. "I have witnessed his use of that gem on occasions too numerous to count, and in each instance his candor met with a none too graceful slap on the cheek and a terse but earned rebuke, yet you tolerate his goading, which will serve you well in your marriage." The partner in nefarious enterprises shrugged. "Else he might beat your bottom raw."

If she had any desire to chastise her intended, it died with the cousin's threat to her posterior. Studying the polished wood surface of the table, she traced the lines of the grain and inhaled a deep breath.

"Mayhap I would, if I were partial to corporal punishments." In a shocking display of familiarity, Arsenius tipped her chin and brought her gaze to his. Then he grazed the curve of her jaw with his thumb. "Alas, I find such barbarity repugnant, so your arse is safe with me."

"Really?" Titus propped on his elbows. "How disappointing for her."

"Perchance I should clarify my meaning, cousin." Trapping her stare, Arsenius eased back in his chair. "I said her arse is safe. I did not say it was immune to my attention."

Heart hammering in her breast, Senara shot upright. "Prithee, may I be excused?"

Folding his arms, Arsenius chuckled. "At last, she speaks."

"And with deference owed to her new lord and master." Titus mirrored Arsenius's stance, and she almost choked on her pride, as she gritted her teeth. "The lady knows her place."

Digging her fingernails into her palms, she stiffened her spine. "It has been an arduous journey, and I am in need of rest."

"Do not taunt the poor thing, as she is correct in her assertion." Titus nudged Arsenius. "I gather she will get little, if any, sleep tomorrow night."

To her surprise, Arsenius stood, rounded the table, and offered his arm in escort. "Come with me, my lady." To their parents, he said, "I will accompany Lady Senara to her chamber and return, forthwith."

She anticipated an objection, but her father merely nodded. In that moment, it dawned on her that she was verily Arsenius's to command, as he owned her, per the King's directive. By his side, the difference in their sizes could not have been more obvious, as the top of her head did not reach his shoulders, thus she abided his wishes, as he led her to the entry, whither the house-keeper lingered.

"Lady Senara retires, and I would show her to her quarters." Arsenius drew Senara toward a narrow passage and a stone staircase.

"Of course, Sir Arsenius." The grey-haired servant curtseyed. "She is installed in the north wing."

In blissful silence, they ascended to the second floor and navigated a winding corridor, until they paused before a heavy oak, double-door portal, which the housekeeper set wide. "Lady Senara, your trunk was deposited in the inner chamber."

A small sitting room, with a large fireplace, opened to reveal a huge four-poster bed and expensive furnishings to which she was unaccustomed, as Papa was a parsimonious sort. Just then, to her unutterable mortification, her belly rumbled.

"Great gulf of hunger." Arsenius burst into laughter, and she endured the ensuing shame with aplomb. "Did you swallow a monstrous beast, or are you in need of sustenance?"

"Sir Arsenius, Her Grace did not raise you to embarrass a lady of character, so you will behave, or I will talk to her." The housekeeper wagged a finger. "Mind your manners."

"Oh, all right, Magge." Duly chastened by the old woman, which gave Senara pause for thought, he shifted his weight. "Bring my fiancée some bread and water."

"Now you have made me angry." Magge rested fists on hips and to Senara said, "I will have maid fetch a fine clarrey, waffres, cheese, and a lovely apple muse." Then the spirited housekeeper turned her gaze on Arsenius. "And if you do not behave, thither will be no perys in confyte for your wedding feast."

"Lady Senara, I bid you a pleasant rest." With an exaggerated flourish, her suddenly contrite groom bowed. Then he stretched tall and licked his lips. "Sweet dreams of me."

"Out, you ill-tempered sack of misery, before I summon Her Grace." Magge stomped a foot. "Lady Senara, I will send two girls to help you undress for bed."

The housekeeper sketched another curtsey and scurried into the hall. Alone, Senara collapsed in a large, comfy chair and exhaled. "What on earth am I marrying?"

CHAPTER THREE

LIFE HAD A way of sneaking up on a man and throwing unexpected events at him, the sum of which Arsenius had always viewed as the excitement in an otherwise predictable existence. But when it came to an unforeseen and unwelcomed arranged marriage, he would settle for an extended stretch of boredom. Or so he thought, until he glimpsed his bride-to-be.

"Wherefore are you so quiet?" Beneath the table in the large family solar, whither the De Wolfes gathered when everyone resided at the Lair, Titus kicked Arsenius's shin. "This is not the raucous celebration we planned in London, is it?"

"Nay, but how could it be, given I marry on the morrow and you the day after?" Arsenius reflected on his bride and consumed another healthy portion of ale. "Lady Senara is not what I envisioned. Although she is beauteous, she is too timid for my tastes, and I baited her with my best hooks."

"I noticed." Titus scratched his chin and yawned. "Commiserations. I can only hope I fare better, in that respect, as I want a woman with spirit."

"Tired?" Arsenius inquired.

"Aye." His cousin stretched his arms. "Your favorite strumpet kept me awake last night."

"You visited Emony?" Of course, Arsenius opted to forgo a carnal encounter so close to his nuptials.

"Well someone had to console her over your impending wedding." Titus arched a brow. "And I cannot believe you rebuffed her request for a final roll in the stables."

"It was time to end the affair, as I am to take the sacrament." Arsenius mulled Senara's demeanor and frowned. "But what to do about my bride?"

"I suppose our mothers can shed some light on the predicament." Titus refilled the tankards and peered over his shoulder. "Whither are they?"

"In the great hall, with our fathers and your in-laws." Was it a Cornish tradition, or were the Arscotts remiss in their duties, to have raised a mouse as opposed to a woman? Dreading his union to the lovely but submissive Senara, Arsenius rubbed the back of his neck. "But Mama promised they would make their excuses and join us, soon."

"What am I going to do if my intended suffers the same affliction?" Upon consideration, Titus drained his tankard. "Mayhap the block is not so bad a fate."

"Whatever happens, we must obey the King's command, not only for ourselves but also for our families." It was the threat to the De Wolfes that ensured Arsenius would keep his appointment at the altar. "We cannot rebel without risking everyone."

"Aye." Again, Titus refilled his mug, signaling his anxiety, as he always overindulged in drink when he was nervous. He glanced up. "Hither they come, as I hear them in the hall."

Mama and Isobeau strolled into the solar and halted.

"Wherefore the long faces?" Isobeau peered at Titus and then Arsenius. "Has someone died?"

"We may as well have, Mama." Titus scowled. "Did you see that lifeless thing to which Arsenius is chained? I hesitate to consider what awaits me, given we know naught of my fiancée, and she is to arrive tomorrow."

"Is that what this is about?" Isobeau laughed. "I thought it a matter of urgency."

"Oh, you gave us such a fright." Mama brushed

aside their concerns with a wave of her hand. "Who would have guessed our big, bad De Wolfe sons are afraid of a couple of gentlewomen?"

"Mama, it is not that simple, and we are not afraid." Arsenius opened and closed his mouth. "But Senara is an abyss of unknowing. Indeed, her eyes are alert, but she sees naught."

"Arsenius Solomon William De Wolfe, apologize, at once." Mama folded her arms, and he was in trouble, as she invoked the full compliment of his names. "No offspring of mine will ever speak thus of a lady."

"I am sorry, Mama." Thither was no time for pride. "But I want a marriage like you enjoy with Papa, whither I might argue with but still love my bride. Is that so wrong?"

"No, my son." Mama pulled up a chair and sat, as did Isobeau. "Yours is a noble endeavor, but it is not so easy as you might think, as you and Senara are strangers, and society views women as property. I wager Senara's fledgling dealings with you are based on the assumption that you prefer the usual arrangement, and you must overcome her expectations to that effect."

"Desi is correct." Isobeau inclined her head. "To

judge Senara on your first meeting is to do her a grave disservice, given the upheaval in her life, which can impact her in ways you cannot fathom." Averting her gaze, she smiled. "How well I recall my initial audience with Atticus. In truth, I was terrified, and I knew not how to address him, given we both struggled with grief over the loss of Titus. But time and patience healed our wounds, and we found incomparable love."

"Thither is no reason you cannot find the same devotion with Senara, if you give her a chance." Mama compressed her lips. "I recommend a period of adjustment prior to the deflowering, that you might acquaint yourself with her preferences."

"That leads to our second question." In haste, Arsenius sought liquid courage and gulped his ale. "How should we...what is the most prudent method...oh, great pit of humiliation, how does one approach and claim a virgin?"

"With care, a suit of armor, and a shield." Mama glanced at Isobeau, and they burst into laughter.

"I am so glad to provide for your amusement." Arsenius propped his elbows to his knees and cradled his chin in his hands. "This is serious."

"Did you ever, in your wildest imaginings, think we

would find ourselves hither, partaking of this conversation with our eldest children?" Mama asked Isobeau.

"Most assuredly, not, as I supposed this was a topic for their fathers to deliberate." Isobeau pressed a fist to her chest and giggled. "Then again, motherhood demands all manner of peculiar duties, without end."

"So you wish to discuss the consummation." With lingering titters, Mama wiped a stray tear from her eye. "Well, if I remember the moment with your father—"

"Prithee, Mama, no details." Arsenius cringed. "I think I might be ill."

"What on earth is wrong with you?" Mama furrowed her brow. "Your father and I are husband and wife. How do you suppose we created you?"

"I know how you managed it, but I prefer to avoid the particulars, whither possible." Arsenius swallowed hard. "A little help would be appreciated, cousin."

Holding his belly, Titus blanched. "I fear I may vomit, thus you are on your own."

"Come now." Isobeau clucked her tongue. "My son is not so delicate, and men are not invulnerable to wedding night nerves. While my first husband, your Uncle Titus, took my maidenhead as anticipated, he was not so assured as you might presume. In fact, he was clumsy but sweet. And Atticus delayed, given I carried his brother's child when we married. When we, at last, came together, it was magic, because our hearts were engaged. Still, it took a while to learn each other's habits."

"And your father was so hesitant he would not stop talking, which surprised me, given we were betrothed from birth and in love." Mama smiled. "But performing marital relations with your wife presents a vastly different challenge, according to my Titus."

"How so?" Myriad options, all of which focused on the physical realm, raced through his brain.

"Because how you begin your life with Senara will determine how you go on, and you cannot just climb atop her and have your wicked way." Mama humphed. "Set aside everything you believe you know about women and resolve to romance your bride."

"Excellent counsel, Desi." Isobeau pointed for emphasis. "Inquire after Senara's favorite foods, especially sweetmeats, and ask the cook to prepare them."

"Bring her flowers."

"Read to her."

"Take her for long rides, just the two of you."

"Talk to her."

"Listen to her."

"Has she any special interests that you might share?"

In rapid fire, Mama and Isobeau assailed Arsenius and Titus with bits of wisdom regarding the fair sex. Soon, Arsenius became muddled in a haze of confusion, until the advice took a decidedly more decadent turn.

"When she is ready, you may sample her most intimate flesh, but you should seek her permission." Mama tapped her cheek. "And confer with her before attempting any deviation from the norm."

"Quite right." Isobeau nodded. "It was months before Atticus and I—"

"No, *no.*" Titus stood and covered his ears. "I am not listening."

"Thank you, Mama and Isobeau." Arsenius ran for the door. "You have been of great service, but that is enough."

In the hall, they tried but failed to ignore the bombastic mirth emanating from the solar.

"That did not go as I had hoped." Titus winced. "Do you think it possible to wash a memory with soap?"

"No." Arsenius shuddered. "Do you recall the night we spent in London, after the Festival of Fire tournament?"

"Aye." Titus leaned against the wall. "Wherefore do you ask?"

A vision of wild and wanton behavior flashed in Arsenius's brain. "You do not suppose our parents have ever—"

"Stop." With a mighty groan, Titus smacked Arsenius. "You had to mention that, as if I am not already gripped in the throes of horror." Wiping his face, his cousin mumbled, "But I am for bed, though I suspect sleep will not come easy for me."

"Rest well." Likewise, Arsenius could not quiet the unsettling whispers wreaking havoc on his senses. Nay, thither was no respite for the weary or anxious. So as Titus set a course for the family chambers, Arsenius steered toward the north wing.

In the narrow passage, to avoid detection he crept. Aye, he crept. Grasping the wrought iron ring at Senara's entry, he slowly pushed open the heavy oak panel and prayed the hinges did not creak.

Inside, the sitting room was dark save the light from the flames flickering in the hearth. But a glow emanated from a thin crack between the inner doors, so he advanced. When he breached the bedchamber, he discovered Senara kneeling on the floor before the fireplace.

"Good eventide, my lady." At her shriek, he chuckled. "You make noise. That is an improvement."

"What are you doing hither? Have you no shame?" Crossing her arms in front of her, she attempted to hide her body from his gaze. Garbed in naught but her thin nightgown, and backlit by the blaze, her shapely curves captivated him. "Get out, before I scream."

"And what will you achieve, beyond further embarrassment, given we are to wed in a few hours?" In the saffron radiance from a candle, her features assumed a more animated appeal, and he adored her fit of pique. "Though I may permit it, as it is remarkably pleasing to hear you say anything."

"Oh, I have plenty to speak on my behalf, sir." She shook her fist, and he wondered if that temper lent itself to other, more intimate activities. "But wherefore have you intruded on my privacy, as it is indecent, given we have not taken our vows? Is it not enough that I am your intended, forced to the altar, despite the fact that I was betrothed to a childhood friend? That my father has lost his home, his title, his fortune, and his dignity? That my family legacy is all but erased? That my people suffer beneath the Crown's iniquitous demands for taxes to pay for a war that did not benefit us? Would you strip me of the last vestiges of self-respect? Am I to bring naught but my flesh to this union?"

"By God's toes, you are glorious in your righteous indignation." Sitting on the edge of the bed, he slapped his thighs. "Tell me more."

"Wherefore should I indulge you?" Then she covered her mouth and sobbed. "And now you will banish my family, condemning them to ruination."

"I beg your pardon, my lady, but you labor under a false assumption." As much as he savored her ire, he had to correct her erroneous presumption. "I have no plans to remove your family from Bellesea. Soon you will be a De Wolfe, and we take care of our own."

"And that protection extends to my relations?" A tear streamed her cheek, as Senara took a single step in his direction. Thither was a strange appeal to her melancholy. "You would guard them?"

"Of course." He shrugged. "It is my duty, as your husband."

With a startling, high-pitched cry, she charged him, and he stood.

Soft, feminine, and warm in his arms, as if she was made for his embrace, she hugged him about the waist and wept. "Oh, thank you. Thank you, kind sir."

"You are most welcome." For that reaction, he would grant whatever she wanted. "So is that wherefore you were so quiet when we met?"

"Aye. Papa cautioned me to hold my tongue." Sniffing, she shifted and retreated from his hold. Smoothing her hair, she collected her robe and covered herself. "I should warn you that I have always been exceedingly frank in my conversations. It is my primary fault."

"Ah, but I consider it your strength, thus you will ignore your father's wise but unnecessary counsel." In that moment, Arsenius found the idea of marriage to Senara far more attractive, so he drew her back to him. "On the morrow, we wed, and we will seal our oath of devotion with a kiss to satisfy those in attendance. So this is for us." Then he bent his head and claimed her lips.

Bedecked in blue, the color of purity, with her hair braided, Senara strolled the walk to the steps of the chapel at Wolfe's Lair, whereupon the families gathered for the ceremony. Hot and cold at once, as she revisited the memory of the tender interlude she shared with Arsenius, she shivered, and her cheeks burned. If not for his assurances, she would have run into the moors, without so much as a backward glance.

Clinging to his promises as a shield against the fear ravaging her senses, she joined her groom. "My lord."

"My lady." Resplendent in his black doublet, hose, and overgown, with his beauteous face clean-shaven, Arsenius bowed. "You are a vision, but I prefer your garb from last night."

"Shh." In light of his shocking comment, she almost swallowed her tongue. "Someone might hear you."

"What does it matter?" Unabashed, he winked. "In a short amount of time, you will be mine, to do with as I choose. If I wish to parade you naked about the bailey, I may do so, and no one can stop me." When she gasped, he covered her hand with his. "Relax, as I am a greedy man, when it comes to you, and no one shall see you thus, except me."

"I am not sure that is altogether comforting." Startled by the prospect, she flinched, as nudity was forbidden in her household. Even when she bathed, she wore her chemise. "Arsenius, you test my patience."

"Get used to it." His response did not inspire confidence, even as the vicar cleared his throat.

"As all parties are present, let us commence the ceremony." Vicar Bernard held high the cross. "*In nomine Patris, et Filii, et Spiritus Sancti.*"

In unison, the crowd replied, "Amen."

In a haze of fear mixed with persistent disquietude, Senara wed Arsenius. When prompted, she played her part and gave the appropriate replies, and at the end of the pomp and pageantry, ownership of her person was transferred from her father to her new husband. Despite their fledgling pact, when he bent to claim his kiss, rightfully owed, she wept.

"Now, now." With his thumb, he daubed her tears. "None of that, my lady wife."

"But I am your prisoner." She sobbed as he framed her face and forced her to meet his stare.

"Nay, Senara." Ever so gently, he brushed his lips to hers. "You are my mate, my other half, my partner in all enterprises. Do you not comprehend the depth of my commitment to you? My heart will be your shelter, and my arms will be your home. Do you think I took that oath in jest?"

"In truth, I have no knowledge of your character and must accept your word as your bond." Had she not promised him frankness? "I mean no insult, but my life is over, and I grieve."

"Ah, but you are mistaken, my dear." In a rush, depriving her of any opportunity to protest, he turned her toward their combined families. "Look about you, Senara. Your life has just begun."

Assailed by the throng, she accepted the well-wishes in the spirit they were offered, but inside she mourned. Wearing a smile as a mask to hide her emotional state, she moved as a puppet on a stage.

"Friends and relations, let us gather in the great hall for food, drink, music, dance, and general merry-making." Atticus drew Isobeau to his side. "I may even be persuaded to join in an estampie."

"Oh, it is always the same." Isobeau swatted at her spouse. "Play an estampie. Play an estampie."

In the massive chamber, Senara met Arsenius's three brothers and two sisters, along with a sea of De Wolfes, De Sheras, and their connections. Seated at the dais, the host and hostess of the Lair presided over the celebration, while Arsenius and Senara were situated at a small table in the foreground.

"Would you like another portion of the sambocade, my lady?" Beneath the table, her husband brushed her thigh with his, and she jumped. "Something bothering you, sweetheart?"

"Are you mad?" The term of endearment struck her as rather forward. Then she reminded herself of their union. "Have you no sense of decency? What of deportment and morals? What of restraint, chastity, and economy?"

"What of passion, or have you never tasted it?" Through their clothing, again he rubbed his leg to hers, and she scooted her seat to the left. Just as fast, he yanked her chair to the right, closer than previously positioned. "You will not escape me, regardless of your attempts, and as your lord and master, I command you to remain hither."

"I know naught of such things." Indeed, the concept was foreign.

"You were betrothed to another for a long time." Arsenius swallowed a huge bite of cheesecake. "Did you never explore the differences in your bodies?"

"How dare you insult me thus?" The very idea made her ill. "I was raised to protect and preserve my honor, for the sake of my future husband. To violate that sacred duty would be to discredit my family, and I would never do that. I would think that you, of all people, would comprehend my actions in defense of our good name."

"You are correct, as I understand more than you realize." In the blink of an eye, his demeanor softened, and he brought her hand to his lips. "I sincerely anticipate feeding you that first taste of pleasure, my treasured bride."

"May I have your attention?" At the dais, Atticus stood. "As the patriarch of the De Wolfes, the duty of the first toast falls upon my shoulders, and I beg your forbearance, as I consider myself a simple man." He shifted his weight. "None of us came to this wedding of our own free will. Indeed, tragedy, conflict, and His Majesty's edict brought us together. This is naught new for the De Wolfes and the De Sheras, as we have endured much strife in our history, but I promise my great-nephew and his bride that all is not doomed."

"To what does he refer?" Intrigued, Senara leaned close to her husband.

"I am certain he will explain." Arsenius kissed her temple, and gooseflesh covered her from head to foot.

"My own union was marked by sadness, as it was preceded by my beloved brother's murder." Atticus gazed at Isobeau, who smiled. "But love healed my wounds, and while the pain of the past is never forgotten, it can be tempered by the incomparable devotion of a soul-deep connection with a right and true mate." He raised high his tankard. "To the Arscotts, I welcome you to the fold. You may have come to the Lair as adversaries, but you leave as kin. Never doubt our allegiance and support, as we stand with you, come what may. To Arsenius and Senara, I wish you the same unfailing relationship that I enjoy with my Isobeau." A chorus of concurrence erupted in the great hall, and Atticus pounded his fist to the table. "Play an *estampie*."

As the first notes reverberated above the noise, the revelers divided into small collectives, joined hands to form a circle, and hopped to the left. The rhythm changed, and the groups rotated to the right. In good spirit, the men hurled insults neither flippant nor earnest, and the ladies laughed, and for the first time since the defeat at Blackheath, Senara rejoiced.

Until she glimpsed a familiar face among the assembly.

As the melody ended, she turned to Arsenius. "Prithee, excuse me. But I should greet my friends from Cornwall."

"Should I escort you?" Arsenius grabbed her wrist.

"Mayhap I should smooth ruffled feathers, before I introduce you, as many lost loved ones to the King's soldiers." At least she did not lie, as thither were those who hated His Majesty and his defenders. "Given the executions of Gof, Flamank, and Audley, I fear what awaits us in Penryn, but I will do my utmost to mediate on your behalf."

"So I am to avail myself of your skirts?" His accompanying smirk conveyed an altogether different intent. "You will protect me against the heathen Cornish?"

"Must you always be so provoking?" She just stopped herself from taking the bait. "Can we never engage in a nice, normal conversation?"

"Sweet Senara, this is normal for me, so you should prepare yourself for a lifetime of provocation." Arsenius bowed and waggled his brows. "But I vow to never leave you wanting."

"I beg your pardon?" In confusion, she blinked.

"Ah, how I adore your blush. Go and receive our guests." Then he claimed a quick kiss and snickered when she caught her breath. "Remember, we are married, thus previously bad behavior is now sanctioned by His Majesty, and I plan to exceed the limits of our license." She swayed, but he offered support. "Relax, as I vow you will enjoy every moment of it."

"You are determined to put me in an early grave." With that, she ignored his arrogant laugh and marched toward the screened passage at the rear of the great hall, whither she located her childhood companion. "Petroc, when did you arrive?"

"Early this morning." Her former betrothed pulled her into an arched alcove. "I am sorry I could not rescue you or suspend your wedding, but I have not yielded the fight." He handed her a folded parchment. "Fret not, Senara. I will liberate you, but until I can enact my scheme, I encourage you to cooperate with your captor and appease that murderous De Wolfe."

"Are you insane?" She checked her tone. "Petroc, I am married. Given I have taken the sacrament, I cannot betray my husband, as he owns my fealty regardless of his past deeds. Whatever your strategy, you cannot succeed whither others failed. Have we not lost enough life? What of your father? Despite his righteous cause, he died for naught."

"Do not say that." Petroc bared his teeth, and he frightened her. "Read the letter, and be ready to act, as I will come for you."

"Wait." Wrenching free, he scowled and plunged into the crowd. In her clutch the letter all but burned her flesh, and she shoved the suspicious missive into her fitchet before rejoining her groom.

"Now do not faint, but we are expected to retire and seal our vows." Arsenius extended an arm, and she settled her palm in the crook of his elbow, lest she topple to the floor. "Wave and smile at everyone, my dear."

"My lord, I am not sure I can fulfill my duties tonight." A bawdy refrain from the men mingled with feminine giggles, as Arsenius and Senara strolled into the entry and toward the stairs. "Prithee, I think I might be ill."

"Calm yourself, my lady wife." Stroking the back of her hand, he led her to the second floor. "As much as I would love to seize your maidenhead, we will not consummate our marriage until we are better acquainted, unless you protest."

"Are you serious?" She came to an abrupt halt. "Or do you play with me, sir?"

"Oh, how I wish to play with you, sweet Senara." He tugged her to his side, and they resumed their walk to what she presumed were the family apartments. "But I would delay, that you might enjoy the singular event."

"And that matters?" She braced for additional taunts.

"It does to me." In that instant, her respect for him grew by leaps and bounds. At a double door portal, he ushered her into a well-appointed sitting room. "Although we defer the deflowering, I require you to share my bed, as we are husband and wife, and I will endure no rumors regarding our relationship. When the time is right, we will join our bodies."

"That is the most decent thing I have ever heard you say." And she knew exactly what to do with Petroc's letter. "Thank you, Arsenius. I am most grateful."

"You are welcome, my dear." With a gentle touch, he caressed her cheek. "Your personal belongings were moved to my chamber, during our wedding feast. If you wish to undress, I grant you the privacy of the inner suite."

"All right." She nodded and exhaled, as she turned and trod into the next room, shutting the doors behind her. Then she ran to the hearth, yanked the missive from her fitchet, and flung the parchment into the blaze.

.

CHAPTER FOUR

A UGUST YIELDED TO September with a vicious tempest, and the leaves changed colors, as Arsenius marked his first sennight as the new lord of Bellesea. After remaining at Wolfe's Lair for Titus's wedding, Arsenius and Senara, along with the Arscotts, departed for the long, arduous, but uneventful journey to Penryn, in Cornwall. Dotted with lush green moors bordered by rocky sea cliffs, with a river cutting through the town, and tall hedges framing the roads, the resplendent Cornish countryside rivaled that of Braewood Castle, his childhood home. But his new residence was anything but excessive.

Conservative in structure, the once grand estate featured a two-story manor house built of red sandstone, with frieze carved parapets and accents composed of the striking black rock unique to the area. Although the house had been fitted with mullioned windows, the roof and several fireplaces were in need of repair, the tapestries were worn and threadbare, providing little in the way of warmth, and food and supplies had been pilfered in Lord Arscott's absence, thus Arsenius's first task was to replenish the stores.

"You ordered prime cuts of beef, Senara?" Sitting in the solar, Ryol perused the account ledger and frowned. "We can subsist on lesser pieces at a substantial savings."

"I asked her to purchase the quality meats, as it is what I prefer." Arsenius studied his bride and admired the curve of her neck. Despite sharing a bed since their wedding, they had yet to consummate their vows, but he intended to change that—soon, before he lost his wits. "And I hired a crew to restore the roof, else we may not survive the winter."

"Mayhap I should delay the additional goods, if economy is a concern." Stunning in her kirtle and matching gown of rich burgundy, which emphasized her creamy flesh, his tempting wife inclined her head and met his gaze, something she did regularly, of late. He considered it a positive sign, in that she no longer shied from his company. Indeed, she sought his opinion on matters of money and his advice on the family business. "What would you suggest, my lord?"

"My dear, at the risk of sounding like a boaster, thither is no threat to our fortune." Perchance, he imagined it, but he suspected she wanted him as he wanted her, as he often caught her staring at him, when she thought him unaware. "Buy what we need, and add a new quilt and bedclothes to your list, that you might sleep in comfort with warm feet."

"Aye, my lord." Her answering smile conveyed she knew just what he referenced, as only that morning she thrust her cold toes to the backs of his legs, and his resulting lurch landed him on the floor. "Should I procure an extra pillow, to soothe aching muscles?"

"That is not necessary, as I believe I have a cure to heal what ails me." In his mind, he envisioned her as she looked last night, when she stood before the hearth, oblivious to the fact that the blaze cast a brilliant outline of her figure beneath her thin chemise. "Are we prepared to meet the local farmers?"

"Aye." Ryol nodded, as the two men had formed what could best be described as a tentative friendship, but Arsenius promised to improve on the relationship. "I think it provident to gather our community and introduce you as the caretaker for our industry. Given your benevolence toward my family, it is the least I can do to ease the transition."

"I am grateful for your assistance, as the difficult circumstances preceding my endowment of Bellesea no doubt fostered hard feelings, and I do not blame the Cornish." In advance of the meeting, Arsenius collected his papers. "In fact, I have a plan that might ease the tax burden, but I can make no promises, and I will explain, in detail, later."

"You would do that?" With an expression of shock, Senara clutched her throat, but it was something powerful in her stare that gave him pause. Reaching through the space between them, some magical force enfolded him in an invisible embrace. "You would intervene on our behalf?"

"Of course." Arsenius rose from his chair and walked to his bride. "The inhabitants of this estate are my charge, a responsibility I take seriously. While I am His Majesty's loyal servant, I understand the horrendous conditions caused by the unfair tariffs, and I would mitigate the situation, if possible. But I shall employ diplomacy."

"You are wonderful." Unshed tears welled in her blue eyes, as she cupped his cheek and covered his mouth with hers.

It was not an aggressive display of affection, as she brushed her tender lips to his, yet did not tease his tongue, but the impact struck him as a lethal blow from his cousin Titus's lance during a competitive tournament. Never had Arsenius enjoyed a more intoxicating kiss.

"I beg your pardon, my lord." The steward knocked on the oak panel, which sat ajar. "Your guests have arrived."

"I should see to the refreshments." Despite her declaration, Senara hugged him about the waist, and he cradled her head. "Thank you, my lord."

"But I have managed naught, yet, my lady." Oh, yes. He would take her. No more delays. No more mornings spent in self-indulgence behind the large gorse bush at the north corner of the house.

"Still, I thank you." Perched on tiptoes, she pressed her lips to his with a loud smack, shrieked, and ran from the solar.

In that moment, Arsenius noted his father-in-law's countenance of surprise. "She is my wife."

"I would say so." Ryol arched his brows. "As never have I seen my daughter so emotional or demonstrative."

"Shall we join the assembly?" In uncharacteristic discomfit, Arsenius shuffled his feet. "I would not make them wait."

A large group of Cornish farmers occupied several tables in the great hall, and a murmur heralded Arsenius's presence. Various glances of suspicion and contempt trailed his every move, as their loss was his gain, but he took no offense. Instead, he resolved to reassure the injured parties and form a mutually beneficial agreement.

"Gentlemen, I am honored that you accepted my invitation." As he had seen his father do on several occasions, Arsenius made the rounds and shook hands with each visitor, out of respect. "Welcome to Bellesea."

That was the moment for which he had been born and bred, the reason Papa required Arsenius to attend the regular agricultural reviews, and why he endured so many lectures on the merits of prudent negotiations. Everything culminated in that single fragment in time, when conflict tested his experience and expertise. Indeed, a leader required more than the skills of a warrior.

And so Arsenius launched into his rehearsed

speech, in a measured tone, which never wavered, even when several men shouted contradictions. Whither they displayed anger, he remained composed. Whither they pounded their fists to the table, he sat relaxed and untroubled. In good spirit, he met every attempt to engage in conflict with imperturbable aplomb, and his plan worked.

Bereft of the dudgeon that drove them to London, and spent of the ensuing insult inspired by the punishment for their crimes against the Crown, the farmers quieted. That was when Senara entered the fray, with an army of servants bearing pitchers of ale, trenchers of roasted ham, cheese, and bread, along with an enticing array of sweetmeats.

With full bellies, the farmers presented a far more cooperative crowd, and that is when Arsenius made his stand. "In light of His Majesty's appointment, I am bound to the people of Penryn, as their guardian. As such, my first order of business is to contact the King and appeal for the royal forbearance. Bellesea is the official producer of Sire's clotted cream, and naught compares to it, else you would have been supplanted by now."

"That is because the process is a great secret known

only to the Arscotts." A particularly vocal gentleman snickered.

"And those of us in possession of parts of that information will take it to our graves," another elderly statesman added.

"I respect your position, and I have made no demands whither the industry is concerned." Arsenius reflected on his notes. "My primary focus is in improving the living conditions at Bellesea, including the construction of several homes, repairs to those structures that require only minor renovations, and initiating labor-saving enterprises intended to increase our combined yield."

Whispers filtered through the throng, interspersed with occasional questions.

"Wherefore would you do that?"

"What do you want in return?"

"How much will that cost us?"

"My friends, and I hope I can call you thus, as I am you ally, the answer is simple." Arsenius stood and splayed wide his arms. "We are stronger, together."

When the farmers took their leave, after consuming profuse amounts of ale, a spirit of camaraderie marked their exit. At his side, Senara assumed her role as lady of the manor, having soothed any lingering doubts by reminding the skeptics that Bellesea was still their community.

"Well that was an exercise in triumph, as you extended charity without robbing them of their dignity." His bride gazed upon him with unveiled admiration, and he cursed the unusual burn of a blush in his cheeks. "Are you busy this afternoon?"

"My lady wife, I am never too busy for you." She bounced with uncontainable excitement, and he decided he enjoyed pleasing her. "What have you in mind?"

Favoring him with a quick kiss, Senara twined her fingers with his. "Thither is something I wish to show you."

⇥⟫⟪⟨

HEELING THE FLANKS of her chestnut mare, Senara set a blazing pace, leaving Arsenius in her wake. Charging north from the main house, she soared past the rear gate and onto the moors. With a light heart, she navigated the verge and followed the path that traced the edge of the sea cliffs.

"Whither are you taking me?" Arsenius drew beside her.

"You will see." She flicked the reins.

To the casual visitor, the trail appeared naught more than a means to tour the vast rugged landscape of Cornwall. In reality, when the dirt lane narrowed and ended amid a cluster of gorse bushes, she veered inland, past a rocky outcrop, whereupon she traversed another walk.

In the valley below, two large buildings and a smaller one sat in the uninhabited wilds of the Cornish countryside, with only the grazing dairy cattle for company. At least, at first glance. But upon careful inspection, even the disinterested would note the well maintained, heavily traveled road leading from the general direction of Penryn.

"Is this what I think it is?" Arsenius arched a brow.

"Aye." Near the primary structure, she drew to a halt and slid from the saddle. "Given your unfailing support, I cannot, in good faith, withhold secrets from you."

"So you trust me with the operation that serves as the sole source of income for Bellesea?" After descending his destrier, her husband took her hand in his, and she squeezed his fingers.

"In truth, I trust you with my life." And no one was more surprised than Senara by that development. "Nay, I did not always feel that way, as I considered you the enemy. But in the time since our marriage, you have been naught but a gentleman and protector. Still, it is your treatment of my people—"

"*Our* people," he corrected.

"You are quite right, my lord." His proprietary demeanor thrilled her to her toes. "It is your treatment of our people that affirms my confidence in you." She opened the door, and they stepped inside the warehouse. "Had you seized my home as an arrogant conqueror looks on the spoils of war, I would have hated you. Instead, you defend my family, you tend the needs of the less fortunate, and you deal honestly and fairly with the farmers, thus I fear you not."

"Senara, I am so glad to hear you say it, as I am no threat to you." The earnestness of his expression further bolstered her position, and she led him to a chamber filled with row upon row of shelving. "Thither are a great many things I would share with you, if you let me."

"I welcome any overture and would meet your proposal, measure for measure, starting hither."

Reaching up, she tamed a wayward lock of his hair and patted his cheek. "According to my family history, our method for creating clotted cream was learned from Phoenician traders visiting Cornwall some thousand years ago, and in that time no one has discovered our process or matched our quality. Needless to say, we take great pride in our wares."

"Very wise strategy, and I do not doubt you." Arsenius bent and peered down the aisle. "What is in the pans?"

"These shallow trays hold fresh milk, and it must be fresh, which is left to rise, from dusk until dawn in the summer, and sunrise to sunrise in winter," she explained. "If you will follow me."

"So that is why you contract with so many dairy farmers." In the heating chamber, he surveyed the massive store of large pots. "And what are these for?"

"After workers collect the whole cream, it is heated to a specific thickness, which every Arscott learns to gauge, and I will teach you, and then it is cooled overnight. What remains is the finest Cornish clotted cream, favored by His Majesty."

"And that is it?" Glancing from left to right, he shook his head. "So simple, yet who would have thought of it?"

"It is a source of great pride." In the final section, whither stacks of small containers filled the area, she snared a receptacle, untied the twine, removed the cloth cover, and scooped the confection with a finger, that she might offer her husband a sample.

Smiling, Arsenius bent his head and licked clean her flesh, and she clenched her gut. "Delicious." He hummed his appreciation. "And the cream is not so bad, either."

To her surprise, he retrieved another taste but smeared the decadent indulgence across her lips, before claiming a searing kiss that curled her toes. Holding tight to her man, Senara struggled to draw breath, as he mingled his tongue with hers, and just when she feared she might swoon, he shifted and broke the connection.

Gasping for air, she struggled with a strange emptiness and an accompanying chill that left her shivering, and she sought solace whither she knew she would find it—in his arms. With something between a sob and a sigh, she flung herself at him, but her knees buckled when he caressed her bottom through her gown and kirtle.

If the preceding kiss had been all consuming, the ensuing one rendered her witless, as a powerful hunger blossomed in her belly, burning in her veins, ravaging her senses, but she knew not how to satisfy the craving. When he released her, she stumbled back and hugged herself.

"What is wrong, Senara?" Arsenius wiped his face and adjusted his doublet. "Did I frighten you?"

"No." She clawed at the neckline of her gown, which seemed to choke her. "I ache, but I know not wherefore I am afflicted."

"Oh, sweetheart." He chuckled and pulled her into his steadfast embrace, and she clung to him. "Let us return to Bellesea, whereupon we shall dine with the family, as is our routine, but do not eat too much. And you will instruct the housekeeper to have a repast of wine, cheese, dried beef, and bread delivered to our solar before we retire."

"Wherefore?" Puzzled by his odd request, she wriggled to meet his gaze, and the heat of his stare only increased her torment.

"Because tonight we consummate our vows."

CHAPTER FIVE

THITHER WERE MOMENTS in life when Arsenius committed every detail, no matter how seemingly insignificant, to memory, as he would forget naught about such special events. As Senara stood before the hearth, garbed only in a sheer robe, with her lush brown locks draped about her shoulders, naught escaped his attention, and he savored the occasion as a fine wine.

"Are you frightened?" He fidgeted with the loose tie of his garment and reminded himself not to talk too much.

"Nay, but if I discover this is a dream, I should be furious." She squeezed together her thighs, and he gritted his teeth. "Is this a dream?"

"It is possible, as you are a vision." Standing, he flicked his wrist and prayed for patience. "Come hither, my dear." Without hesitation, she obeyed his command. Mama, god bless her, had been right and true in her counsel, as thither was no alarm in Senara's visage. "Take off your robe, and turn for me."

Again, his bride abided his request with nary a protest, and he looked his fill, making no attempt to conceal his regard. Indeed, he was a fortunate man. Given what he knew of his lady, had he rushed the consummation, it would have been a battle to end all battles, and he may not have won.

Favoring him with a shy smile, she squared her shoulders. "Prithee, my lord, touch me, as I am cold and in want of your incomparable warmth."

That pedestrian pronouncement almost waylaid his plans, as he wanted naught more than to make love to her. But that evening was not for him. Summoning the finesse that had served him well, he cupped a breast, and with his thumb he teased her nipple, until it hardened to a pebble, inasmuch to divert her while he regained control. "Still chilled?"

She mouthed, *No.*

As he bared himself in similar fashion, she held high her head, ignoring the most obvious difference in their anatomy, the erect length of which paid homage to her beauty in spectacular form. To ease her distress, he brought her palms to rest on his chest.

"Your skin is so hot, like the fires in the cooking room." She splayed her fingers and teased the crisp hair sprinkled about his flesh. "Will you not kiss me?"

"Not yet, else this will be over before we begin." He chuckled, as her furrowed brow betrayed her confusion. "Lay on the bed, my dear."

"All right." To her credit, she stretched across the quilt and closed her eyes.

"Look at me, Senara." He perched on the edge of the mattress. As he dragged the backs of his knuckles along her supple curves in a series of strokes, he gauged her demeanor. "I want you to watch everything I do, so thither are no surprises. And I would have you know thither is no shame in our behavior, as we are married, and our bodies are made to be joined."

Never in his life had he drawn out the experience, had he lingered over the feminine landscape. Rather, he located his mark, mounted her however convenient, gained his pleasure, and compensated the accommodating party, regardless of whether or not she found release.

But for Arsenius, with Senara, her satisfaction reigned supreme.

If he failed to bring her to completion, then he

could destroy the tenuous bond forged, one step at a time, in the months since their wedding, and that would devastate him. So he continued his gentle massage, until she squirmed and wiggled her hips in unmistakable invitation. Only then did he slip his hand between her legs.

"*Arsenius.*" She bucked, but he gave her no quarter, as he found her hot and wet, and he reveled in the proof of her desire. Had he any reservations, she dispatched them with a sigh of unequivocal contentment, and he answered her call.

Working her most intimate flesh in a repetitive cadence, he whispered encouragement and reassurance, and she moaned in accord with his movements. Little by little, her approbation grew, and she yanked his wrist, as if to hasten his attention. At last, he increased his pace, and her expression of adoration mixed with uncontrollable abandon, stark in its clarity, well nigh brought him to tears. The achingly charming scream with which she heralded her virgin release rocked him, and he came alert, in an instant.

In the throes of her intense fulfillment, Senara did not notice when Arsenius loomed atop her, when he gave her his weight, when he parted her thighs, when he set his hips to hers, or when he breached her maidenhead. But when he propped on his elbows, cradled her head, and kissed her, she responded with a passion so formidable, so undeniable, that he could not resist her, and he spilt his seed.

Grunting and groaning, he wrenched with each successive spasm, marveling at the force of his gratification. As he collapsed on his wife, his mind raced to comprehend the level of affinity they achieved, in light of her innocence. Thither was naught unique in the deed, as she possessed the usual parts. Somehow, their union was different. And then it dawned on him—he cared for her. Just as fast, he dismissed the absurd notion.

"Well that was not how I planned our first mating." In search of distraction, he rested his forehead to hers and chuckled. "How do you fare, my dear?"

"Quite well, my lord." She giggled, which tensed her muscles, and in unison they caught their breath. Biting her lip, she gasped. "Is that you?"

"Indeed." Flexing his spine, he withdrew and then thrust, and she dug her fingernails into his shoulders. "Will you teach me what to do, as I wish to please you, that you might never seek another's company?"

"Believe me, sweetheart, you need do naught, and I am yours, unreservedly." Still, he grabbed her knee. "Wrap your legs about me."

Displaying her usual dedication to duty, she hugged him close, followed his instruction, and lifted her ankles. "Like this?"

The position enabled him to attain a deeper connection, as he seated himself fully within her, and he embarked on their sensuous journey with a gentle rhythm. Framing his face, Senara held his gaze, and when he moved, she was with him.

WITH A SPRING in her step, Senara whistled a frisky little ditty as she emerged from her chamber. To her chagrin, the noon meal had been served when she strolled into the great hall, and she promised to do better on the morrow. Then again, that depended on her husband's seemingly boundless stamina.

In the fortnight since they consummated their vows, Arsenius enacted a rigorous routine focusing on a single activity, every morning and night, and sometimes in between, attempting all manner of positions that stretched the limits of her imagination, but she was not complaining. As a result of his robust schedule, she often rose long after dawn, and she fretted that her duties suffered.

"Senara, you are late." Father frowned. "Whither have you been?"

"She performs special tasks, which I deem of utmost importance to Bellesea." Arsenius peered at her and winked, as she understood just what he referenced as a special task. "Sit beside me, my dear."

As had become his custom, her husband opted to forgo his place of honor at the dais in favor of the common tables, which endeared him to the locals. Had anyone thought it an overt attempt to win approval, it would have failed. But Arsenius's genuine nature and unprejudiced treatment of everyone, coupled with his immense stature, emphasized the authenticity of his gesture.

"But I am starved." She yawned, and Papa shook his head. To a maid, Senara asked, "Will you bring me a trencher of poached salmon?"

"Aye, my lady." The servant curtseyed.

Spying a basket overflowing with healthy portions of hot bread, Senara snatched a piece and shoved it into her mouth.

"You are hungry." Arsenius tempted her with a morsel of salmon, which she greedily bit from his grasp, and he laughed. Then he leaned close to whisper, "I know not wherefore you are so ravenous, except I exercised you hard this morrow. Ah, and now you blush, which arouses me, so I shall pay you a visit this afternoon."

"My lord, I must supervise the packing of His Majesty's latest order of cream, else I would indulge you." Beneath the table, he squeezed her thigh through her gown, and she brushed him aside. "Pray, let us delay, that we might enjoy tonight's interlude that much more."

"But I would sample your cream. Do you deny me?" She could never resist his scandalous talk and his precious pout, which he deployed just then. "I could accompany you to the warehouse, and we could divert near the coast and make love behind that large gorse."

"Outside?" she inquired, in a low voice, despite her shock at his ribald suggestion. "Is it done?"

"Thus far, I have taken you in the stable, in the hayloft, in the buttery, and in the rising room, and oh, did I rise for you." He waggled his brows. "What say you, my enterprising lady?"

Basking in the glow of the memories they collected, and the promise of passion, she nodded with enthusiasm. Using his strategy, she walked her fingers to his crotch and caressed his stout longsword. "Cherished husband, I am at your service, unconditionally."

"Woman, you tempt me, even now, and I tremble at the prospect." After claiming a quick kiss, he stood. "Your father and I are scheduled to meet with the town council, to organize the fishermen's relief fund, after the tempest that damaged the boats. Upon my return, I shall summon you for our ride to the warehouse."

"I look forward to it." Just then, her belly rumbled, as the maid placed a steaming trencher before Senara.

"Eat plenty, angel." As he donned his cloak, he pressed his lips to her braided crown. "You will need your strength."

After sating her hunger, she inspected the kitchens and the stores, and then she assisted Mama and Ysella with organization and arrangement of recently delivered supplies and food items. They prepared a variety of jellies, cooked and dried fruits for the winter, and recorded a list of spices and oils to purchase at the market.

"Your father tells me your marriage to Arsenius has

been a blessing, in disguise." Mama covered a container with a square of cloth and secured it with twine. "What say you on the matter?"

"Oh, Mama, I am so happy." Senara pondered the eventides spent in naught but their robes, as they admired the sunset. At dawn, Arsenius never left their bed without satisfying her. "Never have I been so content."

"So he treats you well?" Ysella asked. "Because he strikes me as rather menacing."

"In truth, I am his queen." And never did he let a night pass without reminding her of her place in his world.

"I am astonished." Mama set down a receptacle. "Your affections are engaged."

"Are they?" Senara averted her gaze, lest she betrayed her husband's confidence, but she desperately wanted to believe they had formed an attachment based on sincere devotion. "How do you know, as I can scarcely tell, myself?"

"Do you really doubt it?" Mama clutched Senara's hand. "It is apparent in your face, as you glow, my child. I hope, for your sake, he is an honorable man."

"He is the best of men, Mama." Senara pondered

the bouquet of water pimpernel and heather, to which she was partial, he gifted her, yesterday. "In public, he tends our people as his own and respects the elders. In private, he is kind and gentle."

"He inquired after your favorite flower and foods." Ysella tittered. "And he composed a journal entry as he questioned me."

"That explains the pykes in brasey the cook served at dinner." As well as the potage of roysons with which he tempted her in their bed, and she stifled a snort of mirth. "Indeed, I am a fortunate woman."

As the sun reached its peak in the sky, bathing Bellesea in welcomed warmth, she journeyed with the physic to numerous households on the estate, to provide care for the sick and injured. Even as she tarried, thoughts of Arsenius commanded her senses, and on more than one occasion the physic inquired after her health, which garnered naught but a giggle.

Riding a wave of anticipation, she steered her mare for home to await her husband's desire. In the courtyard, the master of the horse held her mount, as she eased from the saddle.

"My lady, a missive is just arrived for you." The housekeeper curtseyed.

"Thank you." The telltale script on the parchment sent a shiver of dread down Senara's spine. Recalling the note he forced on her at her wedding feast, and that she burned it without reading the contents, she decided not to leap to unsupported conclusions. After breaking the seal, she unfolded the letter.

Dearest Senara,

I am so sorry I could not spare you the unpleasant union to the De Wolfe murderer, and I can only pray for your forgiveness, as I failed you. Prithee, come to the north meadow, near the creek whither we played as children, that we might renew our friendship.

Yours with affection,
Petroc

On the surface, the message appeared harmless, but she knew well her former betrothed and his appetite for trouble. "Oh, Petroc, what do you want now?" In a rush, she flagged the stable master. "Prithee, return my horse, as I must away."

CHAPTER SIX

WITH A LIGHT heart and intoxicating anticipation, Arsenius urged his destrier toward Bellesea, that he might keep his appointment with Senara. After another successful gathering of minds, he broke through some of the more defensive barriers to his position as lord of the estate, and now he looked forward to breaching his wife. It was for that reason, as he traversed the verge, he was surprised to discover his bride atop her mare, galloping to the north.

Whither did she journey without him?

Curious, he changed course and stayed in the down slope, trailing her from a distance. Given the warehouse sat to the east, he knew not whither she ventured. As Cornwall's moors and high grounds were bereft of trees, he relied on the native shrubbery and unique hedges to conceal his pursuit.

At last, she drew rein at a narrow creek, and from behind a large gorse a lone man emerged. When

Senara ran into the stranger's ready embrace, anger flared and surged through his frame, but something else plagued his senses. Pain. Raw and all encompassing, a dull ache settled in his chest, and he wondered if everything they shared was naught but a lie.

Dismounting, he searched for and found a suitable, low-lying branch to which he secured his stallion. On his hands and knees, he crawled closer to his bride and her conspirator, until he could discern their conversation.

"Petroc, have you gone mad?" Senara splayed her arms, as she confronted her former fiancé. "I cannot betray my husband. Not for you. Not for anyone."

Stunned by her declaration, and ashamed that he ever doubted the constancy of her devotion; Arsenius swallowed hard and vowed to make amends.

"You ally yourself with the enemy?" Petroc grabbed and shook her, and Arsenius almost revealed his presence, but his bold bride slapped her friend across the cheek, which set him on his heels.

"How dare you speak to me thus?" Waving her fist, she stretched tall for her petite stature, and he did not envy the unfortunate footpad. "I am the wife of Arsenius De Wolfe, and he owns my unimpeachable loyalty. No argument, however compelling, can inspire me to reward his kindness with disloyalty."

In that, Arsenius concurred, and he promised to kiss her silly when next they adjourned to their chamber.

"I thought you loved me." Petroc's voice cracked as he spoke. "Am I naught to you?"

"Nay, I have always loved you, as a sister loves a brother." Given her proclamation, freely offered without knowledge of her husband's attendance, Arsenius breathed a sigh of relief. "But Arsenius is my life, and he is a good man." In that instant, Arsenius bowed his head. "Talk to him. Share your grievances, and you have my word, as your friend, he will hear you."

All right, he was going to make love to her until she screamed.

"I want naught from him but what the Crown stole from us; our birthright." Then Petroc stared down his nose at her. "Though I should be satisfied with his head on a pike."

"Petroc, I warn you to tread softly." She adopted a familiar formidable pose, and Arsenius actually pitied the fool that tried but failed to menace Senara. "If you take up arms against Arsenius, then you revolt against me, and I will not countenance such treachery, regardless of our longstanding affiliation. I will fight you, with whatever means necessary."

"Oh?" The silk-snatcher sneered. "What do you propose to do about it?"

"I will stop you." She stiffened her spine. "I will defend my husband with all that I am, if you challenge his authority."

For that, he would bedeck her in precious gems of every color. Unaware of the games men played, Senara's confidence threatened her safety, and Arsenius came alert, preparing to strike to spare his bride.

"Indeed?" But as Petroc lowered his chin, she grabbed his ear, and Arsenius bit his tongue against laughter. Whimpering like a newborn babe, her friend dropped to his knees, and she held tight. "*Ouch.* Let go, Senara."

"Surrender your scheme." She remained vigilant.

"Nay." He howled in agony.

"Yield." In silence, Arsenius wagered on his beauteous wife.

"Nay." The milksop yelped. "Pray, release me, and I

shall call my supporters to order on the morrow."

On Petroc's promise, Senara retreated. "And you will cease your nefarious activities, as thither has been enough bloodshed?"

"If you agree to address my compatriots." Petroc narrowed his stare, and Arsenius did not trust the sad sack of ignorance. "They will listen to you, if you wish to avoid another battle."

"Should I vouchsafe your request, you must give me your solemn oath never again to partake of such odious occupations, as it is not wise to bait His Majesty." Mayhap Arsenius would beat her bottom for concurring with the idiotic notion.

"Know that you have it." Petroc nodded, but something in his demeanor troubled Arsenius.

"Then I will see you on the morrow, hither." Aye, he would beat her.

Without so much as a backward glance, Senara reclaimed her mare, heeled its flanks, and steered toward Bellesea. Lingering in her wake, as he retraced his path, Arsenius guarded her brief journey, and she never detected him.

The sun sat low on the horizon when he rode through the gate, and in the courtyard his bride rushed to welcome him.

"My lord, you are late." As was her way, she hugged him about the waist. "I was worried, such that I did not visit the warehouse."

"Demands on my time took longer than I anticipated, angel." As he promised himself, he kissed her—and kept kissing her. "Shall we inspect the rising room tomorrow?"

"I suppose." On tiptoes, she pressed her lips to his. "I missed you."

"Oh?" He rubbed his nose to hers and anticipated her confession. "What did you do, in my absence?"

"The usual minute tasks about the house." With a shrug, she brushed her cheek to his, and he was aroused in an instant. "Would you be averse to dining in the solar, this eventide, as I wish to be alone with you?"

"Of course, my lady." That was not the response he expected. "I am your devoted servant."

"Then I should direct the staff." To his shock, she pushed free. "I will see you shortly, my lord."

Standing stock-still, he admired the gentle sway of her hips. While Arsenius would deny to his death, it hurt him that Senara did not confide in him.

꘎꘎꘎꘎꘎

SPRAWLED ATOP HER husband, Senara caught her breath as Arsenius caressed her bottom. While she had planned to reveal the meeting with Petroc, as well as his scheme to enact a second, smaller rebellion in Penryn, her uncharacteristically quiet spouse pounced on her the instant they gained the privacy of their chamber, and she declared her intent to impart a dastardly plot.

"Now, what was it you wished to tell me, angel?" Was it her imagination, or was he in an unusually playful mood?

"I should begin from the start." Cursing Petroc for creating a divide in her marriage, she lifted her head to meet her husband's gaze. "Do you know of my former fiancé?"

"His name is Petroc Burville, I believe?" Arsenius squeezed her so tight she gasped. "What of him?"

"At our wedding feast at Wolfe's Lair, he approached me with a letter." She tried to ease to his side, but he refused to release her, so she relented. "Given the circumstances of the termination of my first betrothal, I presumed the missive contained naught but nonsense. Since I did not know you, I feared your reaction, and I fretted for Petroc's safety, so I threw the note in the hearth when we retired."

"You did not read it?" He stilled, and she gulped.

"Nay." She shook her head.

"Wherefore?" With his thumb, he teased the curve of her ear.

"Because I married you." Resting her head to his chest, she sighed. "And I took the sacrament. Regardless of the situation preceding our nuptials, I am your wife, till death do us part, and I am compelled by my own beliefs to honor you."

In the blink of an eye, Arsenius rolled her onto her back and engaged in another round of lovemaking that exceeded the first in intensity and tenderness. As he drove into her, relentless in his hunger, he gave her no quarter, as he claimed her lips in a searing affirmation of his desire, robbing her of rational thought.

Again and again, he pushed her to the heights of passion, only to retreat just shy of the sweet pinnacle of their coupling. When Senara feared she could take no more, she dug her heels into his arse, and he rode her, hard and fast, to their special place, whither sight and sound surrendered to touch and feel, until she shattered in ecstasy.

Spent and sated, she closed her eyes and savored the constant beat of his heart.

"So what prompted you to disclose Petroc's letter?" Arsenius shifted to study her face, and she cupped his chin.

"I received a second note, this morning, after you departed for town." Bracing for ire and a possible spanking, she vowed to withhold naught from her husband and accept any punishment. "Petroc bade me meet him, and I abided his request, thinking it naught more than a harmless re-acquaintance between childhood companions."

On guard for the slightest hint of temper, she detailed Petroc's anger and plot to undermine Arsenius, yet her spouse remained calm and composed. So she explained that she promised to make their case to additional Cornish rebels, anticipating an outburst at any moment. Yet the big, bad De Wolfe scarcely fluttered an eyelash.

"And you want me to permit you to grant an audience?" Mayhap she had misjudged his disposition.

"Well, that is what I wish to discuss." She shrugged. "When I agreed to Petroc's demand, it was merely to delay, that I might strategize with you, as I supposed you would know how best to proceed."

"You are wise, as well as beauteous." He pinched her bottom, and she yelped. Then he shuffled to the edge of the mattress, stood, walked to the table in the solar, and filled a goblet with wine. "Thus I am willing to support you, but you will not venture forth, alone. And if he puts his hands on you, again, he will answer to me."

"I beg your pardon?" Seizing on his haphazard admission, Senara sat upright, holding the sheet to her bare breasts. "What do you mean, 'if he puts his hands on me again,' my lord?" When her stronger half turned to face her, his expression belabored a harsh truth she did not want to acknowledge. "Arsenius?"

"I am sorry, angel." With a mighty frown, he sat on the bed and rested a hand to her thigh. "As I arrived at Bellesea, I spied you riding north and pursued you. When Petroc joined you, I feared the worst. Hiding behind the bushes, I relocated to an advantageous position and overheard your conversation."

"So you know everything I said, in defense of your rank." A tear streamed her cheek, and she bowed her head. "You do not trust me."

"Nay, Senara, that is not true." Arsenius pulled her from the covers to sit in his lap, and she slumped against his chest. "I trust you with my life, sweetheart."

"Then wherefore did you not tell me you knew of my encounter with Petroc?" Ashamed, she buried her face in her hands. "How could you let me suffer, given I fretted over your response, as I cherish the attachment we enjoy? Do you think so little of me?"

"But you are blameless, my lady." Then he forced her to look at him. "You and I are quite the pair, as I waited for you to tell me what happened. When you said naught in the courtyard, I mourned the candor that has marked our union, as I supposed you intended to conceal the developments."

"Would you have my confession in the enclosure, whither everyone can participate and offer criticism?" She sniffed, and he kissed her. "That is wherefore I arranged our dinner, hither, that we might strategize without interruption."

"Have I told you how glad I am that I married you?" With his nose, he traced the curve of her jaw. When her husband was aroused, he employed every part of his anatomy to entice and seduce.

"Arsenius, this is serious." Despite her plea, he

pushed her onto the mattress.

"Ah, sweetheart, *this* is serious." With his legs, he parted her thighs. "I want you again."

"But I have a plan." As he slipped inside her, Senara shivered.

"As do I." With his hips, he initiated the delicate dance. "And we will discuss it, later."

CHAPTER SEVEN

THE BRISK SEPTEMBER morrow dawned, and Arsenius and Senara rose early to share the sunrise and review their strategy. After partaking of a light sop and hot tea, they joined Ryol in the great hall, to set their plan in motion. All too soon, he lifted his wife to the saddle of her mare, claiming a kiss to soothe her frazzled nerves.

"It will be all right, sweetheart." As he passed her the reins, he twined his fingers in hers. "I am by your side, even when I am not with you, and naught can harm you."

"I will do my best to avert a crisis." For a while, she met his gaze, and intimate promises, silent but powerful, passed between them. Thither was so much he wanted to declare, but words failed him. Then she nudged her horse and rode beyond the gate.

"Let us depart." Arsenius peered at Ryol. "I do not want her unguarded for the briefest moment."

"My daughter is a spirited woman, possessed of uncommon intelligence, and she will not fail you." Ryol tugged on his gloves. "Remember, she is not alone."

In an unsettling repeat of the previous events, they drove their destriers through the valleys, while Senara crossed the moors. Keeping time in his head, he counted the peaks until she disappeared, and they turned east. As prearranged, his wife lured Petroc and his followers to a hillside, which offered Arsenius the advantageous high ground.

After dismounting, he crawled to the rise to guard his precious bride. When the rebels, mayhap thirty, in all, emerged from the thick bushes, Arsenius clenched his jaw and flexed his fists.

"You came." Petroc scowled. "In light of your defense of De Wolfe, I should not be surprised."

"As promised, I journeyed hither to persuade your supporters to alter their course." To her credit and his infinite pride, Senara maintained her composure. "Prithee, gentlemen, thither is no need for further conflict, and yours is a fight you cannot win."

"But you underestimate the strength of our position, as we have something our fathers lacked." Petroc smiled, and the hair on the back of Arsenius's neck stood on end.

"And that would be—what?" she inquired, as her horse shifted.

Licking his lips, Petroc advanced. "A prisoner."

When the boothaler dragged Senara from the saddle, she screamed, and Arsenius lurched upright and revealed himself. "You dare touch my wife?"

In an instant, hell broke loose, and the group unsheathed their weapons.

"De Wolfe." Baring his teeth, Petroc situated Senara as a shield, but that would not save him.

Moving swift and sure, Arsenius drew, aimed, and threw a dagger, which embedded in Petroc's shoulder. In the ensuing commotion, Senara broke free and ran into Arsenius's waiting arms.

"You should not have come hither, on your own, *loyalist.*" Petroc wrenched the knife from his person and spat.

"Who says I am alone?" Cradling his wife's head, Arsenius peered to his rear, as a large collective of farmers marched forth, over the rise. "It would appear you are outnumbered, Burville. Surrender, and I will let you live. Revolt, and I can assure your demise by my hand."

"Austol, is that you?" an elder called.

"Breok, what on earth are you doing?" another De Wolfe ally shouted, with unmasked disgust. "Would you bring shame upon your family? Come hither."

One by one, the would-be rebels relented, until only a few stubborn combatants remained. Bleeding, Petroc clutched a sword. "De Wolfe bastard, I challenge you."

"I am only too happy to oblige, Burville." As Arsenius leveled his weapon, Senara hurled herself into the fray.

"Nay, my lord. I forbid it." Wrapping her arms about his waist, she refused to relent. "If you are injured, I will never forgive you."

"You are worried about me?" That stunned him, as he presumed her display of concern was for Petroc's benefit. "But I am His Majesty's soldier."

"I do not care, as I will not risk a single hair on your head." Then, to his utter amazement, she framed his face and kissed him. "I love you."

"Sweet Senara, I love you, too." And naught could spoil his amity, as he wore her treasured declaration as a suit of armor. "Now stay behind me, angel. Indeed, I need no sword to triumph over your former fiancé." To Petroc, Arsenius said, "Fortune smiles upon you, as my lady has just bestowed upon me a gift without equal, so I shall be merciful and let you live. But I intend to teach you a lesson, so let us have done with it."

With a pathetic lunge, Petroc made the opening advance, which Arsenius deflected with ease. When the boy who would be a man cut to the left, Arsenius sidestepped and smacked Petroc upside the head. In a comedy of errors, the younger opponent executed a series of clumsy maneuvers, all of which failed to meet their aim, but Arsenius humored the lad. However, when he glanced at Senara and noted her tears and expression of terror, he indulged Petroc in a final move. To wit Arsenius kicked the incompetent fool in the arse and simply stole the sword from Petroc's grasp.

"Yield, Burville, as you test my patience, and my wife weeps." Arsenius winked at Senara, and she sobbed, before he returned his attention to his adversary. "Cede or die, the choice is yours."

"I surrender." Petroc grimaced and rubbed his injured shoulder.

"I accept." To Ryol, Arsenius said, "Send the others home, take him to the physic, and see that he receives proper care. When he is healed, bring him to the house, as I gain far more use from an ally than a corpse."

"Of course." Ryol nodded.

Facing Senara, Arsenius bent and swept her into his arms, and she burrowed to his chest but said naught. Instead of conveying her to the mare, he lifted her atop his destrier, leaped into the saddle, and settled her in his lap. Spurring his destrier, he set a blazing pace for Bellesea.

By the time they passed through the gate and drew to a halt in the courtyard, he was just as emotional as his bride. Without a word, he lowered her to the ground, and then he descended. Absent a prompt, his wife turned aside, in perfect positioning that he might carry her, which he did.

In the main entrance, they met the housekeeper, and Arsenius glanced at Senara. Ah, how well he knew his bride. "Have the ancere filled with warm water, as her ladyship desires a bath. And have dinner served in the solar, as we do not wish to be disturbed."

"At once, my lord." The servant scurried toward

the kitchens.

At the double oak panel entry of their suite, he kicked open the portal. In the relative quiet and privacy of their sanctuary, he set Senara down. In an instant, she charged him and burst into tears.

"It is all right, my heart." Aye, he would make love to her for the remains of the day, but at that moment, he needed to hold her. "I was never in danger."

"You could have been killed." Lifting her chin in unmistakable invitation, she closed her eyes, and he brushed his lips to hers.

Standing at the windows, he reveled in her soft and feminine body, as below the courtyard came alive with activity. Resting his cheek to her braided crown, he sighed in unimaginable contentment, as he opened the door to his memory and let her declaration command him.

Even when the small army of servants appeared, bearing steaming buckets of water, Arsenius refused to let go of his wife, and she made no protest. Alone, at last, he untied her laces and loosened her gown, which dropped to the floor. Then he removed her kirtle, hose, shoes, and chemise.

In silence, he led her to the large tub and held her

hand as she eased into the water. After stripping bare, he joined her. Sitting at the end of the ancere, he spread wide his legs and pulled Senara to rest against his chest. Dropping back her head, she nuzzled him and sighed.

It could have been an intensely seductive exchange, marked by the customary grunts and groans and licentious release, but it was not. Indeed, their passion had far surpassed the superficial pleasures of the flesh, unrivaled by the base desires and shallow attachments indicative of the physical realm. Theirs was a connection based on the invisible but unshakable devotion, impervious to human weaknesses, when two hearts, in perfect accord, were engaged, and thither was no doubt that Senara was his match.

"Tell me again." Arsenius kissed her temple.

"I love you."

Thither were no more words spoken that night.

THITHER WAS HELL to pay for the previous day's fledgling rebellion, and as Senara reclined in the solar and reviewed the plans for the feast of Michaelmas, in November, Arsenius met with various community leaders to address any lingering grievances. At times, loud voices echoed off the walls in the great hall, but she pretended not to notice. When a particularly startling outburst rattled the windows, she closed her ledger and marched into the corridor.

As she strolled into the massive gathering room, she found the men kneeling in a circle on the floor. Of course, naught should surprise her, as she was a De Wolfe bride. Raucous cheers pierced the quiet, and the group shouted all manner of confusing encouragement. She located her husband and peered over his shoulder, only to discover they raced four large beetles. Just then, Arsenius noted her presence, and he surrendered his spot to a rather enthusiastic spectator.

"How are you, my heart?" How she adored his term of endearment, employed in the glow of their mutual declarations.

"Wonderful, now." He cupped her cheek, and she turned to press her lips to his palm. "And you?"

"Every moment spent in your company is paradise." His expression sobered. "Did you sleep?"

"A little." Although she considered herself a strong sort, witnessing his fight with Petroc terrified her, as she could not contemplate life without Arsenius, and horrible nightmares plagued her slumber. "But I rest better with you at my side."

"Go upstairs and climb between the sheets." Patting her bottom, he kissed her forehead. "I will join you shortly."

"Do you not have business to conduct?" As always, she wound her arms about his waist. "I do not wish to be a burden."

"Your father can finish it, and you could never be a burden." After a comforting massage of her back, he set her apart from him. "Do as I say, sweetheart. Anon, I shall arrive to guard you."

"If you insist." In obeisance of his request, she turned toward the main entry but paused in the doorway of the great hall.

It was only in June when she sat in that chamber and lamented her impending nuptials to Petroc. Then the Cornish lost the Battle of Blackheath, incurring the Crown's wrath, and she was given in marriage, as a spoil of victory, to Arsenius. Never could she have predicted how that decision would change her life.

Owing to her husband, Bellesea had been restored to its former glory, with improved windows, a roof that did not leak, and new tapestries. The stores were always full, the community was always tended, and laughter always filtered through the estate. And just last week, he broke ground on a new warehouse, which would double their yield of clotted cream.

As she ascended the stairs and navigated the passage to their private quarters, she reached behind and tugged at her laces. By the time she closed the oak panel of their inner suite, she had loosened her gown enough to pull it over her head.

Given her husband's stated preference for nudity, she stripped bare before slipping between the soft bedclothes. When she settled amid the pillows, he appeared and all but ripped off his garments, but he was gentle as he scooted beside her, beneath the covers.

"Do you know that I was scared of you when we first met?" She rolled onto her side and shifted close, resting her head to his shoulder, as he scratched her scalp. "In my defense, you are rather large, in stature."

"And now?" He drew the quilt to her chin.

"I long to have our child." And she wanted a large family. "And I feel safe only in your company."

"It will be my pleasure to help with that." As had become their custom, they held hands even in bed. "But as of this moment, I want you to recover, as you had quite a shock. Then, you have my most earnest promise that I will apply myself to begetting our first babe."

"I shall hold you to it." She yawned and stretched her legs. Closing her eyes, she recalled her conversation with Mama, the day Papa returned from London, and her world shifted on end. Basking in the warmth of her husband's beauteous body, she pondered her union, as the relaxing lure of sleep beckoned.

Nay, Senara's marriage to Arsenius was not perfect, but it was much closer to perfect than she ever thought she would achieve. Although he had no connection to her past, they did not spend their childhood in each other's company, and they were strangers when they took their vows, he knew her better than anyone, and he loved her. While she was his, he was, most definitely, hers, and by his side was whither she belonged.

EPILOGUE

A SHRILL SCREAM of agony pierced the thick tension in the solar, echoing off the stone walls, and Arsenius raked his fingers through his hair, groaned, and stood. Focusing on the ceiling, he inhaled and exhaled, summoning calm. A second gut-wrenching shriek left him shuddering, and he clasped his hands behind his back and paced before the hearth. Telling himself to be strong, to persist in the face of misery, he flexed his jaw. The third howl of unfathomable torment had him marching to the entry of his bedchamber.

"My son, do not interfere in women's work." Father rested a palm to Arsenius's shoulder, as various shouts of encouragement rose from beyond the oak panels. "I know it is difficult to withstand the thought that you brought such suffering upon your wife, but it is the way of life, and she will survive."

"But Senara has labored for hours." Gritting his

teeth, as his better half let loose a startling crescendo of pain, he vowed never to touch her again. Just as quick, he quashed the speculation, as she was temptation personified, and he could never resist her. "How much longer must I endure this affliction, as it is killing me?"

The cry of a babe brought all activity to a halt.

Holding his breath, Arsenius locked forearms with his father, and Papa's muscles flexed, betraying his tremulous state. For what seemed an eternity, a commotion ensued, and then the child's squall grew louder and more impressive.

"Ah, that is a De Wolfe." Beaming with pride, Papa chucked Arsenius's chin, and only then did he sigh in relief. "The first of a new generation."

Just then, Mama opened the door. Always the picture of elegance, she lifted her chin. "You may come inside, if you wish, and meet your firstborn."

Without hesitation, Arsenius rushed to Senara's side, as she remained in the birthing chair. Kneeling, he brushed aside a lock of hair from her damp forehead and kissed her. "How are you, my angel?"

"Wonderful." She smiled and nuzzled his palm. "And you?"

"Better, now that I know you are all right." To his

dismay, he bent his head and wept. "I was so worried I might lose you, and what would I do without my heart?"

"But I am fine, and thither is someone I would like you to meet." She flicked her wrist, and a maid brought their bundle of joy, swaddled in a blue blanket, to Senara. As his wife cradled the infant in a secure embrace, she glowed with unveiled elation. "My lord, may I present your firstborn and heir. Your son."

The lump in Arsenius's throat almost choked him.

"Talan Titus Ryol De Wolfe, in honor of his Cornish heritage and our sires, as we decided." So many emotions invested his frame, as he leaned forward, claimed Senara's lips, regardless of those present, and rubbed his nose to hers. Indeed, no one could shame him for loving his bride. "You have made me so very happy, and I love you."

"And I you." Amid the excitement and gushing family members, Senara yawned. "Sorry, my heart, but I am tired."

"Arsenius, wherefore do you not repair to the great hall and celebrate this momentous event with the men, while we bathe Senara and put her to bed, that she might recover?" Mama reached for his son, but

Arsenius retreated.

"By all means, tend my beauteous bride, but I shall remain in the solar, until you are finished, whereupon I will guard her rest, as I am reluctant to leave her, and you may take my son to the nursery." He strolled into the outer room. "However, at this moment, I would become acquainted with him."

"Of course." Mama nodded and returned to Senara, as servants hefted steaming buckets of water to fill the ancere.

Holding his precious treasure, Arsenius gazed at his father and fought to find the words to express his triumph. "Is he not beauteous…incredible…"

"He is all that and suit of armor." Papa sniffed, and thither was not a dry eye in the vicinity. "And I am a grandfather."

"As am I." Ryol wiped the wetness from his cheek. "This is a glorious day, which must be suitably marked."

"I could not agree more, so let us adjourn to the great hall and commence the festivities." Papa slapped Ryol on the back. "I, for one, am in dire need of a drink."

"An excellent suggestion, my friend." Ryol laughed,

as they ventured into the corridor, debating myriad expectations for Talan's future. "Mayhap we can indulge in some of Hedra's roasted ham, as I am starved."

Alone with his son, Arsenius walked to the window overlooking the courtyard. "One day, after I am gone, all of this will be yours, and you will uphold the traditions that have long defined your estimable ancestors." The babe cooed, and Arsenius chuckled and hugged his heir. "First, you must grow and learn about life, and I will teach you to ride, to wield a lance and a sword, to fight, to fish, to hunt, and, most important, how to treat a lady." His child gave vent to an adorable snort, as if to declare some innate skepticism. "What? You do not believe I possess sufficient expertise in that area? Well, just ask your Mama, as we created you, and I hope we produce several brothers and sisters, that you might never be lonely. For now, let us commence with a history lesson, because, as my father explained to me, to understand whither you are going, you must know from whither you have come. Thither was once a formidable knight known about the kingdom as William De Wolfe..."

ABOUT BARBARA DEVLIN

Bestselling, Amazon All-Star author Barbara Devlin was born a storyteller, but it was a weeklong vacation to Bethany Beach, DE that forever changed her life. The little house her parents rented had a collection of books by Kathleen Woodiwiss, which exposed Barbara to the world of romance, and Shanna remains a personal favorite. Barbara writes heartfelt historical romances that feature flawed heroes who may know how to seduce a woman but know nothing of marriage. And she prefers feisty but smart heroines who sometimes save the hero, before they find their happily ever after. Barbara earned an MA in English and continued a course of study for a Doctorate in Literature and Rhetoric. She happily considered herself an exceedingly eccentric English professor, until success in Indie publishing lured her into writing, full-time, featuring her fictional knighthood, the Brethren of the Coast.

Connect with Barbara Devlin at BarbaraDevlin.com, where you can sign up for her newsletter, The Knightly

News. And you can find a complete list of books on Barbara's Amazon Author Page.

Facebook: facebook.com/BarbaraDevlinAuthor

Twitter: @barbara_devlin